# Trusting the Plan

*Sunrise Beach - Book 2*

## Charlotte Golding

# The Sunrise Beach Series

This series is all about Stella Britton and her life after scandal and divorce. Stella is starting over in a new town away from the city she once loved. She hopes to come to love the small beach town she's chosen and that she and her daughter will find a new life away from the whispers.

Relationships have ups and downs, ins and outs. Stella knows this all too well. Now she'll navigate difficulties with her daughter, cherish a new friendship she didn't expect, and learn to depend on her neighbors.

Can she do this new life thing? Of course! Will it be easy? Not on your life!

# Trusting the Plan

## Sunrise Beach - Book 2

### Charlotte Golding

# Chapter One

Stella Britton was trying hard not to stare at the customer who had been in her gallery for nearly an hour at this point, trying to decide what he wanted to purchase, if anything at all. She was getting better at feeling people out, if she did say so herself. Most people preferred for her to stick close by while they shopped, so they could ask questions about the art, and so she could tell them any stories about the paintings with which they were spending a particularly long time. A few, however, found this to be overbearing and tedious.

Luckily for Stella, the few who shopped this way were normally folks who just wanted a few random pieces of local art to hang in a waiting room or cafe. The only thing they really cared about was that the color scheme matched the room they were picturing, so they were able to shop fairly quickly. The ones who spent a long time here typically were interested in both the art and in Stella herself.

This man, however, was the worst of both worlds. He wanted to silently stare at each piece for an unreal amount of time but did not want her help or input. Honestly, she had no idea what was even going through his head if he wasn't curious about the art's creation. How could he possibly spend so long in here without saying a single word?

"Is there anything I can help you find?" she asked. The question felt stupid because everything she had was right there on the walls. It wasn't like the local grocery store where one could walk around looking for a particular item forever. It had taken her months to figure out Mr. and Mrs. Jeong's organizational system at the convenience store.

The man looked up and smiled. "I think I've made my decision," he finally said. Stella could have sighed with joy, but she fought the urge.

It wasn't as if she were an impatient person normally, she thought as she helped him get his selected painting down from the wall. He'd chosen a painting of a grove of trees.

"This is actually in my hometown," she said idly while she looked through her binder for the price. Each painting was priced a little differently, depending on how much time she'd spent working on it.

"Oh," said the man, entirely disinterested. She had forgotten, momentarily, that this man would not care about her story, but she found her mind wandering to it anyway.

Her parents owned quite a bit of land in a little town called Trussville. They weren't rich, not by any means, but there was a lot of dead space in the whole town, land that wasn't owned by anyone. There had been a lot of it behind their home growing up, and it led to a small forest. As a child, she'd never been allowed to play there. By the time she was a teenager who probably could have obtained permission from her parents, she hadn't wanted to. When she thought about the house she'd spent her childhood in, one thing she remembered most was that she could go out the back door and see, in the distance, the grove of trees that served as the entrance to the forest.

Stella had painted the grove after she'd gone back home to Trussville for her parents' funeral. She'd thought the painting would be more difficult to part with, but she found it almost cathartic to sell it. Looking at it made her sad.

As the man took his painting and left, Stella was relieved. She finally had time to paint the image that had been nagging at her brain for the past hour. She'd been gathering her paints and canvas when the man had walked into the gallery.

Though she never liked to do so, Stella flipped the "open" sign in the window to read "closed." If another customer came in, it might alter her mood. Whether that change was for better or worse, it would change the final product, which she wanted to ensure came out exactly as she was envisioning it.

Ever since she'd received a voicemail that morning from her mother-in-law, Gwen, she hadn't been able to stop thinking about the divine emerald ring that Gwen had always worn on her right hand, opposite her wedding ring. It had belonged to Jeff's great-grandmother and was the only nice thing she'd ever owned. Gwen had refused to take a penny from Jeff once he'd started bringing in millions. She'd said that it was because she had everything she could possibly want already, and Stella had admired her for her strength at the time. She'd wondered if she could have resisted such an offer, in Gwen's shoes.

It had turned out to be a blessing that Gwen hadn't taken anything because she hadn't lost anything when the IRS had revoked it all.

Gwen Britton was a wonderful woman. Even after Jeff had been arrested, her relationship with Stella had remained strong. She and Stella often talked on the phone, and though Stella had originally told herself she was calling to ensure that Gwen was doing all right in the wake of everything, she'd found that their chats had been just as beneficial to Stella as they were to Gwen.

As if summoned, just before Stella could sit down to begin painting that gorgeous emerald ring from memory, her phone rang with a call from Gwen.

"I'm sorry I missed your call this morning," she apologized after the short greeting. "I was jogging and had my headphones in. How are you, Gwen?"

"Don't worry about a thing," Gwen reassured warmly. "I've been well, sweetheart. How about you? How's the life of an artist? And Kelsey?"

Stella laughed. "Oh, stop. Kelsey and I are both good. She's busy with midterms, and I've just been trying to keep up with the gallery. It's amazing how many people heard about it just from the exhibit."

"That's lovely, Stella! I've been meaning to ask you if you would mind me coming down to see it sometime."

A grin broke out over Stella's face. Her mother-in-law had been a sort of surrogate parent after her own had passed when she was young, and there was a childish pride in her that felt excited to show Gwen what she'd worked so hard on.

"I'd love that. Anytime."

"What about the weekend after this one? The eleventh? Do you have anything special planned for then?"

Stella was shocked. "That soon?" she asked. "Is something wrong?" Gwen was not, by any means, a person who liked to fly by the seat of her pants. She was meticulously organized and liked to plan even the smallest events as far out in advance as possible.

"No, no, nothing like that," she promised. "I've just been missing you lately. I want to see you, and it's not like I've got much else going on."

Gwen and her husband, Matthew, had split when Jeff was a child. Their relationship was rocky at best. They'd done their best to co-parent, and they still managed to look past their resentments and be civil at holidays and funerals, but they really weren't on speaking terms. Now that Stella was going through it herself, she had a new appreciation for Gwen for forgiving Stella for sitting them at the same table at her wedding. She wasn't sure that she would be able to be so kind to Jeff if she were face to face with him again. Gwen was an emotional person in every way, but that was the one area in which she did demonstrate some restraint.

"You're always welcome here," Stella said. "Next weekend works perfectly. I'll let Kelsey know."

The two said good-bye, and Stella hung up the phone, feeling a familiar stress headache building around her temples. With the gallery finally booming, it certainly wasn't the best time for her to be entertaining, but she supposed it was a blessing in some ways, too. Kelsey would be on her fall break, which meant that she wouldn't fall behind in classes if she wanted to hang out with her grandmother, and that she had no excuse to hide behind if she didn't. Stella had made more than enough to pay that month's bills, so she didn't have to worry about taking a few days off from the gallery, and the weather was finally perfect for sightseeing.

Stella supposed she was being selfish to resent the timing. She would find the time. After all, family was the most important thing to her, and she really did miss Gwen. It had been far too long since they'd last seen one another, and it would be nice to catch up. She'd just have to make sure she dusted the house and checked to see if they still had their old air mattress, so she didn't have to ruin her back sleeping on the couch.

When Stella arrived home, Kelsey was taking a break from studying to make a grilled cheese sandwich in the kitchen. Stella had rarely seen her this week because of her study schedule, and she smiled as she set down her purse and keys.

"Hey, you," she greeted. "I was wondering if you still lived here." Kelsey groaned and let herself be hugged by her mother.

"I'm tired," she complained. "I'm so ready for fall break. I've written way too many essays this week."

Stella held her tighter. "You're almost done," she reassured. "I'm proud of you."

Kelsey pushed her sandwich from the pan onto her

plate and grabbed a handful of cherries from the refrigerator for a side. "How was the gallery? Sell anything?"

Stella nodded as she took over Kelsey's pan to make her own sandwich. "I did," she said. "Actually, I wanted to tell you I heard from your grandma today."

"Oh," Kelsey said, her tone flat. "How's she doing?" The question was forced, as she clearly didn't want to be talking about her. Kelsey and Gwen had been close all through her life, but her tune had changed after Jeff's embezzlement scheme was made public. Stella remembered how hard it had been to win her daughter's trust back after everything, fighting against the resentment that Kelsey held toward her for not having figured it out sooner.

"She's good. She wants to come visit next weekend."

Kelsey stopped chewing to gape which almost made Stella laugh out loud. "She's coming here?"

"Yes," Stella replied. "Why? Is that okay?"

Kelsey shrugged in that teenaged way that meant that she was upset but too proud to admit it. "It's fine," she said. "Just unexpected. I thought I was going to get to enjoy my break, but seeing Grandma is fine, too."

Stella sighed. "Be nice," she commanded. "What happened with your dad was not her fault."

Kelsey shifted in her seat. "I know," she finally accepted. "It's just hard to think about seeing her. He always talked about how much she spoiled him as a kid, remember? Grandma gave him everything that he wanted. That's just the only reason I can think of for him to steal money from his work like that."

"He did that because he decided to," Stella reminded her. "It's no one's fault except his own, and it's certainly not

Grandma's. I know she's a little... much sometimes. But I really want you to try to get along. Maybe even have fun."

Kelsey rolled her eyes. "I'll get along," she compromised, "but I draw the line at having fun."

"Hopefully, you'll change your mind," Stella laughed. Kelsey stood from the table, trying hard not to show that she was feeling irritable.

"I think I'm going to take my dinner into my room. I can do some review stuff while I eat."

Stella nodded, not wanting to push her into talking. That never went well, and besides, Kelsey would be okay. She never did well with sudden changes in plans, but she would come around. At least, Stella hoped that she would. Hopefully, the lessons she'd learned in forgiving Stella would transfer to her grandmother and seeing her again would bring back fond memories rather than difficult ones.

"Okay. I'm here if you need anything."

Kelsey said good night which meant that she wasn't planning on coming back out of her room that night, and Stella sat at the table to eat her grilled cheese sandwich by herself. She thought of the emerald ring she so wanted to paint and how the plan would likely have to wait until after Gwen left.

# Chapter Two

Stella was not able to resist the pull of painting the emerald ring even though it meant that her house would likely be criticized for being dusty, and she might have to sleep a few nights on the uncomfortable sofa. She hoped that the painting would be worth the pain.

The gallery was open, as she didn't want to start rumors that she was going out of business by closing it for longer than she had to in order to visit with her mother-in-law. However, she hadn't seen a customer all day, which was fine, she thought. Her paintings were selling sometimes as quickly as she was able to make more, which was a great thing, but it did leave the walls feeling a little bare at times. It wasn't the look she had envisioned for her gallery, but she hadn't had the time to think about creativity when she was so focused on the idea of painting lessons.

At the art exhibit she'd held a few months ago, several people had taken down her business phone number for art lessons. She hadn't been so sure she was even interested in offering them at first, but the idea had grown on her. She'd taught her good friend, Adelle, after all, and that had been so much fun that it had never even felt like work. Of course, she didn't expect all her classes to be like that one, but maybe she would like it more than she thought. Not to mention, it might be a chance to meet some new artists from all over the area and even stir up some conversation about her own work while she promoted her students.

The painting of the ring took hours out of each day for three days, but when she finally decided she was finished, she found that it looked just how she had wanted it to. Her depiction of the ring was exactly as she remembered it. Stella was a little nervous, even if irrationally so, to see the real thing in person the following weekend.

In the meantime, Stella cleaned her house like a madwoman. Living with Jeff in Atlanta, they'd entertained all the time. She even had a cleaning staff that came in part-time to help her, especially when Kelsey was younger. It gave Stella a chance to focus on things like being on the PTA, supervising each field trip, helping with every class party, and taking Kelsey to do fun and enriching activities on the weekends.

It wasn't as if Stella or Kelsey were messy people, but they were comfortable with a space that looked like someone lived in it. Beds didn't always have to be made, books could stay on the coffee table while they were being read rather than returning them to the shelf, and if vacuuming the floor happened a day or two late, that was all right.

Gwen was not of the same opinion. She liked a very

clean environment. Almost sterile. When Gwen would visit, Jeff had always been tense, demanding that everything look perfect before she arrived. Though she knew Gwen would never be rude to her, the thought of her judging Stella's home made her feel just guilty enough to put a little extra time into dusting and sweeping.

By the time Gwen Britton arrived at their home a week and a half later, the place was relatively clean. It had given Stella an excuse to give her bedroom a little attention. She'd neglected to decorate it with anything because she figured that she was the only person who would be in it. At the time, she'd had to think about her budget so much that she'd just decided it wasn't worth the expense. But with the gallery doing as well as it was, she could afford to splurge. She purchased some nice picture frames and filled them with photographs of herself and Kelsey and used them to decorate the bare dresser. Interior design had never been her passion, but by the time she'd finished tying the remaining decorations and photos on her wall with a beach theme, she thought it didn't look half bad. Hopefully, Gwen would agree.

Normally, Stella would have made Kelsey come with her to pick up Gwen from the airport on the morning she arrived, but because the plane had arrived before seven in the morning on the Saturday after Kelsey had finished her finals, she'd decided to show a little mercy and let her daughter sleep in as late as she wanted.

Stella hadn't had any reason to go to the airport since she'd said good-bye to Adelle and her husband, Peter, a few months ago. Pulling into a parking space at the top of the parking garage brought back some sadness, but she shook it off and headed down to the airport terminal to wait for Gwen. The plane had just landed, so she was sure that it wouldn't be long before it began to unload its passengers.

As soon as she saw Gwen, Stella broke into a grin, raising her hand as high as she could to wave and hopefully stick out from the crowd of others bustling around the small airport. "Gwen!" she called when her mother-in-law began to look around for her in the crowd.

"Stella!" Gwen replied, rushing toward her, her carry-on bag in tow, to envelop her in a hug. "It's so good to see you, honey. How have you been? You look exhausted."

Stella smiled. She was used to this. Gwen was a bit of a busybody, and Stella had prepared herself for it. "I'm good," she replied. "Just an early morning. It's a bit of a drive from our house. How was your flight?"

"It was fine," she replied as she allowed Stella to take her carry-on bag. "Not too terribly long."

"That's good. Are you hungry, or did they serve breakfast on the flight?"

"They did, but I didn't eat. Plane rides always make me a little nauseated. I could use a cup of coffee, though."

"Done. We'll find a coffee shop or something on the way home."

Stella listened to Gwen talk about the flight for the few minutes it took for them to get to the car. It wasn't complaining really, just something to fill the time since they didn't want to get into anything real or important before they could sit in private and talk. She'd missed this. The feeling of having a family again came on stronger than ever as she loaded Gwen's carry-on and luggage they'd stopped to get from baggage claim into her car.

Gwen had been like a mother to Stella after her own mother had passed away when she was just a young adult. She had been dating Jeff at the time, since the two were high school sweethearts, but they weren't even in their twenties yet. Jeff had been incredible at supporting her at the time, but if it hadn't been for his mother, Stella wasn't sure she'd have made it through that horrible year. Gwen had been working at the time, but she'd cashed in all her vacation hours to make sure that someone was constantly with Stella for the first few weeks of adjusting to her loss. When Jeff wasn't able to be with her because of college classes or work, Gwen was always there to bring her food and water even when Stella didn't want to eat or drink. Gwen had been the first person to open Stella's curtains, just a crack, after she'd spent the first three days after the funeral in bed in the dark.

Slowly, with deliberate care and so much love, Gwen had become like a second mother to her. Even after the acute pain of the loss had started to ease, Gwen had never been one to shy away from acting like a mother figure to her. She'd taught Stella to cook, to sew (even if she wasn't any good at it), and had always been there to give advice when she needed it. All of that came rushing back when Stella saw her, and she was overcome by fondness and love.

Stella pulled over to a coffee shop she'd never been to before, and the two went inside. It appeared the shop also sold pastries and sandwiches, and Stella ordered a blueberry muffin along with her latte. Gwen had sworn she didn't want anything other than coffee with a little sugar, but she didn't protest when Stella had ordered her a croissant, too, with the hopes that it might settle any lingering nausea from the flight.

The shop was mostly empty, save for the workers and one young man in the corner doing work on a laptop. They picked a table and sat down. Stella thought Kelsey would be glad for the delay anyway. It gave her a little more time to sleep in and get ready for the day.

"Really, how has it been living on the beach?" Gwen asked. "It sounds so glamorous, but from what you've told me over the past months, I'm not so sure."

Stella sighed. She hadn't even been aware that she'd been describing this place in such a negative tone for the first months.

"It took a while to adjust, I think," she said. "I was mostly just bitter. I didn't want my life to change. Kelsey didn't want to move, and she was miserable when we first got here. We were always at each other's throats and that, combined with everything else, was frustrating. I felt like I couldn't do it all on my own."

Gwen looked sad, though her smile didn't falter. It was in her eyes. "I understand that," she said. "I wish you hadn't had to do it on your own. I'm so sorry for—"

"Gwen, no," Stella curtailed. "It's not your fault. You were dealing with a lot, too."

Gwen nodded. Just talking about this topic was hard for her. Stella couldn't even imagine the idea of Kelsey doing something like what Jeff had done. The conflicted emotions Gwen must be feeling, wondering if she had done something wrong or if she could have done something differently to avoid this outcome. The pain of having a child, even a grown one, in prison must be incredible.

"It's just been hard," Gwen admitted. "I miss him."

Stella nodded. "We all do. Are you still visiting once a week?"

"At least. I think it's been helpful for me. I don't think I'll ever understand why that boy did what he did, but at least I can get what was going through his head at the time a little better. I needed that."

Stella nodded. "I'm glad it's been helpful." For a moment, she was tempted to ask about Jeff. A part of her that still loved him, if not as her husband then as a friend and the father of her child. She cared that he was doing well. However, every time she tried to form the words, her anger got in the way, and the thought that he deserved whatever was coming to him for what he did to her family prevailed over her concern. Gwen seemed to sense that and smiled.

"He's okay. He knows what he did was wrong, but that doesn't mean you need to forgive him yet, honey. You can take the time you need to heal because he really hurt you. He was in the wrong."

Stella was grateful for her understanding. There had been so little of that empathy in Atlanta. Everyone she knew had wanted to put themselves in her shoes, but none of them had actually done so with real concern. They all imagined themselves in Stella's situation with righteous superiority, swearing that if they had been in her place, they'd have figured it out sooner or worked it out internally rather than filing for divorce. That had only fed into the rumors that she had been a part of it, painting her as a criminal mastermind who left her poor, manipulated husband as soon as he went to prison for her. Thankfully, Gwen had always had the good sense to ignore those tabloids.

"Do you ever miss him?" Gwen asked, a question that took Stella by complete surprise. She hadn't really allowed herself to think about whether or not she missed Jeff. He was gone from her life, and how she felt about it wouldn't change that.

"I... don't really let myself miss him, I suppose. I try not to let myself think about it too much. I get so angry when I do."

"I understand. I know things were hard right after everything came out."

"Hard?" Stella laughed bitterly. "I didn't think I was going to get through it at all. I thought my life was over. What Jeff did... I don't understand. It ruined everything."

Gwen nodded. "I know. I still hold a lot of resentment, too."

"We had the perfect marriage, the perfect kid. Our life was going so well, even without the money. We didn't need any of that to be happy."

"He thought he was going to make things better. He wanted the best for Kelsey."

"Yeah, well, look where that got him." Prison. Divorced. No contact with his child who wanted nothing to do with him and couldn't forgive him after tearing apart their family. She took a deep breath to calm herself. Regardless of what she felt toward Jeff, this was still his mother, and she loved him. Gwen had been punished more than enough for a crime she had no part in committing. "You know, things have actually been pretty good here in

Sunrise Beach. I think you'll like the community. There might not be a lot to do, but it's not too far of a drive from some nice tourist attractions. Plus, the beach is lovely."

Gwen waved this off, as if she weren't terribly interested, forcing her demeanor to shift back to light and airy. "That's all well and good, but it's not why I came to visit! I just want to spend time with you and your sweet daughter. How has she been handling the divorce? And having her daddy in prison? I can't imagine it's been easy."

Stella frowned. "Well, it definitely has not been easy," she agreed, "but she's been really brave. It was hard at first, but things have gotten better. Some of it was just that I needed to learn to meet her halfway. Once I started to do that, things got a lot better for the two of us."

"That's wonderful," Gwen said. "And how's she been doing in community college?"

The unspoken disappointment behind the words "community college" made Stella's heart hurt. Of course, Kelsey's above-average intelligence and promising future that could have possibly extended beyond their means was the catalyst for the entire embezzlement scheme. It might not have been why Jeff had kept it up for so long, but the desperation to form a sizable college fund for Kelsey had been a factor in why he'd started. She'd been on the path to attend an Ivy League school, and now Kelsey had had to completely rearrange her plans for her own future. It had been heartbreaking, even if she'd barely complained about it. Even in her anger, Kelsey had known that was something that was too sensitive to talk about and had never once blamed her mother for the fact that she was getting a two-year degree from a local school rather than a four from a prestigious university. Her dreams of having coffee before class on the Harvard campus had been dashed, but she'd been relatively upbeat about that part of things at least.

"She's at the top of her class," Stella said proudly. "She had midterm exams all last week, so she's been stressed, but of course she knocked them all out of the park."

Gwen nodded approvingly. "Well, we all knew that was going to happen, didn't we? That girl is too smart for her own good." Having eaten most of the croissant, she stood from the table and drained her cup of coffee. "I can't wait any longer. I just have to see her!"

Stella took her own half-finished coffee with her as she led Gwen back to the car, where she fell asleep due to exhaustion from the long flight. Stella was left alone with the soft hum of the radio for the half hour it took to drive the rest of the way home.

Kelsey was, thankfully, awake when Stella came through the door. She'd been hoping that she wouldn't have to wake her up since Kelsey was a grumpy riser.

"Kelsey!" Gwen greeted loudly, seeming to have recovered from the drowsiness of her nap as soon as she laid eyes on the home. "It's been so long! I've missed you. Come here!"

Kelsey plastered a clearly-fake smile onto her face as she complied, hugging her grandmother for an amount of time that Stella could tell was longer than she wanted. "Hi, Grandma," she greeted in return. "It's nice to see you. How are you?"

"I'm wonderful, now that I've seen you," she replied. "I heard you're doing well in school. Making lots of new friends?"

Kelsey would have rolled her eyes if that question had come from Stella, but she resisted the urge, possibly because of the warning glare that Stella shot over Gwen's shoulder as she wrestled the luggage through the door from the trunk of the car.

"Uh, yeah," she replied. "I am."

"I knew you would. A gorgeous girl like you, of course everyone wants to be your friend. I'm sure you've got people trying left and right to spend all their time with you."

Kelsey chuckled awkwardly. "I don't know about all that, but I've met a few nice people. We study together on the weekends. Sometimes, we go to the mall."

"I'm so glad to hear it. I worry about you, you know. Both you and your mom. I think about you all the time."

Stella decided that Kelsey would be fine to handle the conversation unsupervised while she dragged the luggage into her own bedroom and set it on the floor. She had no idea what Gwen could have possibly brought to make her luggage so heavy, but she knew she was going to feel the pull the next morning. With one final lamenting look at her bed that she would have to surrender for the next week, Stella allowed herself only a moment to sit and breathe before returning to the living room.

Kelsey and Gwen had made their way to the sofa and were chatting. Kelsey actually looked invested in whatever Gwen was saying, a fact for which Stella was grateful. She'd felt guilty that she had pretty much taken over Kelsey's entire school break with this unexpected visit, so at least she was hopefully having some nice conversation. Not wanting to intrude, Stella made her way into the kitchen and grabbed herself another small cup of coffee from the pot that Kelsey had apparently started that morning. One cup was simply not enough. While Kelsey and Gwen gabbed in the other room, Stella took her time sipping her coffee.

"Oh, that's just how he's always been, though," Stella heard Gwen say once she was no longer fighting to hear over the noise of her own rustling around. "I always used to say that your father had this need to be the biggest fish even if he was in the smallest pond. Whatever he did, he always wanted to be the best at it. It didn't even matter if he liked it."

Kelsey laughed. "I didn't know we were alike in that way," she said. For a moment, there was a part of Stella that wanted to go in there and put an end to this conversation quickly. Kelsey had only just gotten past her dad leaving, and now Gwen was going to come in and tell her all these stories, making him seem so sympathetic and human? How would that affect Kelsey? She couldn't imagine that it would be good for her to begin feeling sorry for her father, or worse, to begin siding with him on the entire crime.

"Oh, I see a lot of your dad in you," Gwen said loudly. "You're definitely his child, that's for certain."

"In what ways?"

That, Stella decided, was enough for now. Before Gwen could reply to her question, Stella went back into the room to join them. It appeared as though Gwen knew that she wasn't meant to be talking about this because she stopped as soon as she saw Stella.

"So, have you put any thought into what you want to see first?" Stella asked. "The beach is right there, and it's a gorgeous day. The weather is supposed to be nice all week, in fact."

Kelsey did roll her eyes, now. "Yeah, they always say that. Then there's a freak storm."

"Well, that's true," Stella had to admit. "That's just coastal life. The weather is a little unpredictable."

"I have, actually, decided," Gwen said. "I would really like to see your gallery, if that's all right."

Stella was a little taken aback. That wasn't something she'd anticipated Gwen taking an interest in. When she'd paint while married to Jeff, Gwen had always seemed a little judgmental about it. She'd always gone out of her way to remind Stella that it was not a career but a hobby. She'd done it more politely than that, of course, but the sentiment was there all the same.

"Really?" she tried and failed to hide her surprise.

"Yes. I've heard so much about it. I had no idea that your hobby was going to be so successful and lucrative. I'm excited to see what you've put so much work into!"

Stella nodded. "Sure," she said, "we can visit the gallery. Whenever you feel like you want to go. Don't feel like there's any rush. I know it's been a busy morning."

Stella had to admit that she was a little nervous to show Gwen the gallery. If she'd known that Gwen had actually meant it when she'd said that she was interested in seeing it, she probably would have put some of her paintings in the back. The ring, for example. She was a little embarrassed at the thought of letting Gwen see that one.

There were few paintings of Atlanta left in the gallery. In fact, there were few paintings left in the gallery that were hanging up when she'd first moved into the space.

Things were moving so quickly, especially because of the art show. She'd sold quite a few pieces that night. She was a little glad they were mostly gone. Paintings of the beach, which Gwen didn't know by heart, would be subject to less criticism than the ones done of her hometown, of the sights she'd grown up seeing.

Stella decided to hope for the best. She was constantly surprised at how well people responded to her art, and she had to hope that her mother-in-law would be the same.

# Chapter Three

For a while, they sat around the house drinking tea and chatting. Gwen told stories about her life in Atlanta, stories that Stella would have envied a year ago. Before she'd retired, Gwen had been the owner of a salon in Atlanta. It was nothing fancy, but she'd had full control over everything. Though some might have found it annoying how often she told the story of working her way up from sweeping the floors to cutting hair to taking ownership of the place when the owner sold it, Stella couldn't get enough. It was the kind of freedom she had wanted at the time, and not only that, Gwen had earned it herself. Stella couldn't help but admire that.

Kelsey didn't look nearly as impressed by the tale which was understandable, given that she'd heard it so many times before. Gwen had semi-retired when she turned sixty, working part-time doing bookkeeping and other various jobs around the salon. Now, five years later, she had finally fully retired. She'd even sold the salon, which had given her quite the nest egg to live on for the rest of her life, especially combined with her retirement fund.

"That's why I was so eager to come down here and visit," she explained. "I know that working at the salon is too much for me now, but the retired lifestyle just isn't for me. Where's the excitement?"

"You have to make it yourself, I think," Kelsey suggested. "I always thought that retirement was kind of, I don't know, like, your time to do whatever you wanted to do that you didn't have time for when you had to work. If you spent your days at your desk wishing you were out fishing instead, go fishing. Stuff like that."

Gwen was gazing at Kelsey with admiration, and she looked surprised. That was something Stella loved about watching older adults talk to Kelsey. They were always shocked by how intelligent she was.

"You're too wise for your age; does anyone ever tell you that?"

Kelsey smiled sheepishly. She wasn't great at taking compliments yet. Stella wasn't sure that Kelsey fully believed people when they told her how amazing she was. It wasn't that her self-esteem was terribly low, it was that Kelsey was so smart she couldn't even see how intelligent she really was.

"Well, I learn everything from my mom," she said. Stella could have teared up right there, but she held strong.

"Oh, you're much smarter than I ever could be."

It was true, Stella thought. Kelsey was already surpassing her in so many ways. She was in college, something Stella hadn't had the opportunity to do. Her parents had passed right as her graduating class was beginning to make decisions about what they wanted to do for the rest of their lives. Stella hadn't had the foggiest idea, if she had been honest with herself. Part of her wanted to do something big, like becoming a lawyer or a doctor, but she'd wanted a family as soon as possible, and Jeff had been just as into the idea of getting married right out of high school as she was. In hindsight, she really should have waited and figured herself out first.

Then, while she was over at the house of one of her friends for a sleepover, her entire life had changed for the first time. It had been a rainy Friday night. Her parents had decided to go out to dinner, and their car had skidded off the road while Stella was out with her friends. Neither her mother nor her father had survived the crash when the car had rolled down a short embankment and into a ditch. That night, the state troopers had shown up at her friend's house and, in front of everyone at the party, told her that her parents had passed away and that the troopers were going to take her home.

She barely remembered anything about that night from that point on. Really, that whole week was a blur of tragedy and being busier than she'd ever been in her life. Luckily, the funeral arrangements hadn't fallen to her, as her parents' siblings had taken over those tasks. Jeff had been there for her, but he clearly hadn't known what to do or say. There was nothing he could have said that would have made things any easier.

Gwen had broken their house rule and allowed Stella to sleep over at the house, as she was too distraught to return to the family home. Under normal circumstances, Gwen was strict about that, ensuring that Stella was home by the time she went to sleep even if she had to drive Stella herself. After the accident, though, things had changed a bit. Gwen had opened up a futon in the living room and told Stella that she could stay as long as she wanted. She'd cooked for her, talked to her, and held her while she cried. Gwen had an uncanny ability to know when Stella woke up from a nightmare, crying silently for her parents at the age of just nineteen. Without fail, she always "just happened" to be getting up to make herself some hot chocolate in the middle of the night, and she always made a cup for Stella, too.

It wasn't the same as having her parents, and she'd have given anything to have them back. But to this day, Stella believed that the love from Gwen was the only thing that carried her through the worst thing that had ever happened to her.

She'd stayed with Gwen until she and Jeff moved out to get a place of their own. That was a big part of why they married so young. She felt restless and knew that she couldn't keep living with her boyfriend under his mother's roof, but she also had no other place to go.

"I think I want to see the gallery soon," Gwen said, pulling Stella from her thoughts. "We could go for lunch first. Does that sound all right?"

Stella smiled, reminiscent of all those terrible, yet so well-loved, days of her life. "That sounds perfect. Do you like deli sandwiches? I know of a really great food truck that parks along the beach at this time of day, pretty near the studio."

·  ·  ·

Gwen was open to the idea of having deli sandwiches on the beach for lunch even if it wasn't her usual go-to, and she ended up loving what she'd ordered. Stella had already known that she would. She recommended this place to customers at the gallery all the time, and there wasn't one person who hadn't come back and raved about how good it was. She maintained that it was one of the best restaurants in Sunrise Beach, and it didn't even have a ceiling.

After lunch, Stella and Gwen went to the gallery. She walked around looking at the paintings for a while, though not as long as some of her customers had spent with them. She had never been the artistic type, and Stella supposed she was just grateful that Gwen was showing any interest at all. After all, she'd reassured her that it wasn't necessary, but she'd insisted on coming to visit.

Stella had all but forgotten about the painting of the emerald ring until Gwen stopped in front of it, and Stella felt her face heat up in embarrassment. She felt a little judged, as Gwen gazed for a long time.

"This is my ring," she said, and it was not a question. At least Stella had managed to paint the image she was going for, she thought.

"Yes," she admitted. "I, uh, hope that's not weird. I just always thought it was so pretty. Whenever I think of my teenage years, that ring is in my head. I'm pretty sure you only took it off to shower and to sleep."

"I'm just surprised it was something you'd want to paint," Gwen admitted.

"It means a lot to me because you mean a lot to me."

Gwen smiled at that, taking Stella's hands. "You've

always been like a daughter to me, Stella. I really hope you know that."

Stella nodded. "Nobody can ever replace my mom," she said, trying not to get choked up, "but you were there for me in a way no one else could have been. I always felt like I missed my mother, but that in some ways, I still had one."

That made Gwen teary-eyed as well, and she took a deep breath, laughing a bit to ease the emotions of the moment. "Well!" she exclaimed, drying her eyes with one careful thumb to avoid smudging her makeup. "This was wonderful, dear. It's really a beautiful little place you've got here. The gallery and the beach."

"Thank you," Stella said. "Now, I'm sure you're exhausted from such a long day. I texted Kelsey, and she said she'd watch a movie with us at home if you're interested."

"I can't think of anything that sounds better."


The next morning, Stella woke to the alarm she'd set on her phone and immediately turned it off. She'd ended up not having time to find the air mattress after all, and there was no way she was going running after a night spent sleeping on the couch. She sat up with a stifled groan.

"Ugh," she complained aloud. She hadn't slept on a couch since the last time Kelsey was grounded for missing curfew. Stella had been so worried that she'd stayed up for hours past her normal bedtime. She eventually fell asleep on the sofa only to be woken up by Kelsey coming through the door several hours late, citing that she'd lost track of time and that her phone had died. Jeff's level head had been the only reason Stella hadn't already reported Kelsey missing, and she was grounded for so long afterward that she had never, ever made that mistake again.

Still, aching back or not, Stella knew that Gwen was an early riser like herself, so she allowed herself only two (okay, four) presses of the snooze button before she finally dragged herself up and to the kitchen to put on a pot of coffee.

When she began to hear rustling from the back bedrooms a few minutes later, she assumed that Gwen had woken up and that it was safe to start breakfast. She hadn't wanted to wake her mother-in-law, but she also didn't want to cook a stack of pancakes only to have them go cold. As she took flour, sugar, and baking soda from the pantry, she heard footsteps coming down the hallway and was surprised when she heard the voice of the person making them.

"Wow, homemade pancakes? It's been a while, hasn't it?" Kelsey asked, and Stella smiled.

"It's a special occasion."

"We used to have a special breakfast every Sunday, remember? Before—well, you know. Everything."

Stella nodded, remembering those times. Throughout Kelsey's whole childhood, Stella had made homemade breakfasts once a week, either pancakes or French toast, complete with bacon, eggs, and toast. She'd always really looked forward to it, even though it was a big mess to clean up, and they always ended up having the sub-par leftovers for dinner when she made too much. Stella had always thought it was better to have too much than not enough.

"Did you hear whether or not Grandma is awake?"

"I think so," Kelsey replied. "I heard someone bustling around in your bathroom, so unless we have gremlins, I'm pretty sure she's doing her hair."

"Hopefully, she's almost done," Stella said, feeling less optimistic than she sounded. Gwen was a classic Southern woman, heavily inspired by Dolly Parton. While she didn't like the glamor of Dolly's look in the slightest, she did love the big hair, and had been doing it the same way since the early 1980s. Even though Stella had seen Gwen's hair down and relatively straight in the early years she'd spent with Jeff, she could barely picture it if she tried.

"Maybe the smell of pancakes and bacon will motivate her to finish up," Kelsey suggested, and Stella rolled her eyes even as she moved to get a bowl. If she had to choose between a hungry teenager and a mother-in-law who had to reheat her pancakes in the microwave, she'd choose the latter every time.

"Something smells delicious," Gwen announced as a greeting when she finally came into the kitchen nearly ten minutes later. Stella had already burned that tricky first pancake and was adding to the stack while bacon cooled on paper towels.

"I'm glad," she said. "It might not be Southern home cooking, but it's the best I can do."

Gwen sat at the breakfast bar beside Kelsey, smiling. Her hair was, indeed, looking perfect—short and brown well past the years when the color was natural and permed. Stella could practically smell the hair spray over the aroma of breakfast.

"How do you like your eggs?" she asked. When the

consensus was "scrambled," Stella cracked half a dozen into a bowl and set to work, trying not to think about how many pans she was using. She didn't even know she had this many dishes in the house.

Breakfast was, as usual, a relatively quiet affair. They chatted lightly as they ate and sipped coffee. Stella turned on the news, so she could watch the weather.

"It's supposed to rain, according to my phone," Kelsey said, and the lady in front of the greenscreen map confirmed it.

"Aw," Stella lamented. "That's no good. I was hoping we could go to the beach today."

"That's all right," Gwen said. "We can use the day to see the town. What do you normally do for fun?"

"Oh!" Stella exclaimed. "I can't believe I didn't think of this sooner. A good friend of mine owns a tea shop on the other side of town, and it's really lovely. I think you'd have a good time there. Any interest in checking that out?"

Gwen agreed enthusiastically. She loved tea, and Stella was sure she'd enjoy the shop even more. It was owned by her friend, Felicia, whom she'd known for a few months and had grown close with despite the short amount of time.

"I'll let her know I'm going to bring you by this afternoon. I'm sure she'll reserve a table for us."

# Chapter Four

Stella was correct in her assumption that Felicia would save her a table, and she was glad that she did because the place was full to capacity. Sundays were the tea shop's busiest days, as people liked to come after church to sit and talk in a relaxed environment.

The shop, called the Townsend Cafe after Felicia's surname, was on the side of town opposite Stella's gallery. It was one of Stella's new favorite places in town. The interior was decorated with a classic, rustic look that still appeared modern with wooden chairs and tables featuring vases of fake flowers. Bonsai trees adorned the counters, and Felicia had added fake ivy around a few surfaces to give the place an even more mystical appearance like she was about to have tea in an enchanted forest.

"Is that your art up on the walls?" Gwen asked, pointing at one of the walls. Stella was about to be impressed with her ability to have spotted it when she noticed that two of them were parks in Atlanta, and that was likely what Gwen was recognizing rather than Stella's unique art style.

"It is," she said. "That's actually how I met Felicia. She came in to buy art for her shop when she renovated it a few months ago, and we hit it off. She invited me to the grand reopening, so I could see my paintings on her walls. We've been friends ever since. I come up here pretty often."

"Aw, that's so sweet," Gwen said. She was clearly not quite as excited to see Stella's paintings on the walls as Stella herself had been, but she supposed that was natural. No one could probably be as excited as she had been.

"Stella!" A bubbly, British voice came from behind her, and she grinned.

"Hi, Felicia," she greeted, allowing Felicia to mime kissing her on each cheek—something that had taken Stella a while to get used to but now found somewhat charming. "It's good to see you."

"Back at you," Felicia said. "And this must be your mother-in-law. I'm Felicia Townsend. It's lovely to meet you."

"Gwen Britton, and likewise. I love what you've done with this place. It's really gorgeous."

Felicia broke into a wide smile, showing her perfect, white teeth. Stella wondered how she could drink so much tea and still have teeth that practically sparkled. "I've heard so much about you. Now, Gwen, is that short for Guinevere? I'm a bit of a fanatic for the Arthurian legends."

"Gwendolyn," she replied, and Stella could tell that Gwen was becoming a bit overwhelmed. Sometimes Felicia, with her high energy and the way she focused all her attention on the person with whom she was speaking, could make people feel that way.

"You saved us a table, right?"

She nodded. "Yes! Right this way. I've so much I want to talk to you about!"

Stella laughed. "Me, or Gwen?"

"Both!"

Felicia led them to a table and sat across from Stella and Gwen, not needing to be invited to feel welcome. She handed Gwen a small menu from the table, knowing that Stella had it memorized and always ordered the same thing. She'd branched out a few times at first, but once she'd found a favorite tea, mint, and tried a slice of their butterscotch pie, she'd never strayed. The employees sometimes started getting her order ready when they saw her car.

"So, tell me about yourself," she asked Gwen. "I've heard so many good things."

"Oh, that's sweet of you to say," Gwen replied. "There's really not much to tell. I'm retired. I used to own a salon."

"That's so lovely. You know, I think it's wonderful that you and Stella remained so close even after the separation. I hope that's not a weird thing to say."

"Not at all," Stella reassured. "Gwen is like a mother to me. I'm lucky she stayed around because I don't know what I'd do without her."

"Stella is like the daughter I never had. I still love her, and nothing could change that."

"You two are so sweet," Felicia smiled. The waiter came around to take their orders and food was on the table in no time at all. In the meantime, Felicia told the story of how she came into possession of the tea house. Stella, of course, knew the story already. Felicia had come to Sunrise Beach from Manchester, England, a few years ago on a whim. Well, that wasn't quite true. Her older brother, Graham, who was her best friend and the person she looked up to the most, moved to Sunrise Beach on a whim, and she moved with him. For a while, they'd shared an apartment, but they'd been able to separate once the money started coming in. Graham worked as a business consultant while Felicia built up her tea shop. By some miracle, they'd both been extremely successful.

Graham had since moved to Manchester to care for their ailing mother and had been living there for the past two years. However, their mother had passed six months ago, and he no longer had to remain tied to the home. She knew that Felicia missed him terribly, as he hadn't been able to travel in all the time he'd been looking after their mother.

"I'm surprised that this business is as popular as it is," Gwen said after hearing her story. "I mean no offense by that, just that tea isn't as popular here as it is in Europe. Americans tend to prefer those super sugary coffee drinks, the ones that taste more like milkshakes than coffee."

Felicia laughed. "Don't I know it," she agreed. "I was worried about that, but I think that ended up working in my favor a bit. There were no other businesses around quite like mine, and people were curious. We have good food and good tea, and last year, I finally caved to the pressure and started selling bottled soda from the refrigerator for the people who just can't get behind the subtlety of tea."

"That's the thing I love most about it," Gwen said. "The flavors are usually not so forward and in your face.

You have to spend your time with it. Not to mention the health benefits. I've been drinking at least a cup of tea every day for forty years, and I'm healthier than I was when I was a pop-fiend teenager."

"I wasn't the biggest tea person before I met you, Felicia," Stella interjected, "but it's grown on me."

"Yes, you never liked the green tea I used to make."

"It tastes like grass clippings! I maintain that."

Felicia giggled. "At least you finally found something you could drink without dumping a cake's worth of sugar into. Oh, Gwen, you should have seen her when she took a sip of the first tea I brought her. It was a lovely black tea flavored with turmeric and ginger. I thought she might like it because it's warm and spicy like a gingerbread cookie."

"I'm guessing she didn't?"

"She spit it out."

"I did not!" Stella laughed. "I *choked* on it. That's different."

Gwen was laughing now, too, and Stella allowed herself a moment to absorb the peaceful atmosphere while her new best friend and her mother-in-law chatted lightly. She couldn't have hoped for this to have gone better. The two were getting along even more than she had expected them to, which was saying something, because she'd already thought they had a lot in common. Not to mention, Felicia was one of those bubbly and warm people who could make friends anywhere she went. She'd been exactly what Stella had needed after her first close friend in Sunrise Beach, Adelle Christen, had gone back to her home in New York. Stella liked to think that perhaps because Felicia was missing her brother, that

Stella had been just the person that Felicia had needed, too.

When their food came, they were already so caught up in conversation that they barely even registered it being set in front of them. Felicia had that power over people, sometimes. Stella supposed that it was partially because of her accent. Gwen was curious by nature and even more so into the lives of others. At worst, she could be a bit of a meddler or a little nosy, but it was always with the best intentions and usually harmless. For her, meeting someone like Felicia, who had countless tales of growing up abroad, attending an all-girls boarding school and sneaking out to kiss boys in Alexandra Park and being chased away by the night guards when they were caught, was entrancing. Felicia loved to reminisce about her childhood and young adulthood in England, so it was a match made in heaven.

"I was even more intolerable when I went off to Uni," she recalled after swallowing a bite of her food. "I don't know how my poor mother put up with me. If she knew half of what I got myself into at University, I think her heart would simply give out. She'd never look at me the same way again."

Sadness, raw and deep, flashed across Gwen's face, and though she tried to mask it, Stella could see it plain as day. Felicia had no idea that Gwen's son had committed crimes and was in prison, and if she did know, she likely would have chosen her words more carefully. Stella longed to do or say something that would make her feel better, but she was afraid that the damage was already done. Gwen rallied and smiled with a melancholy expression that made Stella's heart hurt for her.

"A mother always loves her children, no matter what. I'll never understand why you children put us through what you do."

Though it was said with a jovial, jesting tone, Stella could hear the pain behind it even if Felicia couldn't. Stella reached out under the table and took Gwen's hand, squeezing it comfortingly.

"If I put Kelsey in an all-girls boarding school, I don't think she would ever speak to me again," Stella said, breaking the tension.

"Kids these days!" Felicia joked. "Boarding school should have been good for me, I think, but it only made me rebel more. I'm just glad I settled down once I graduated from Uni. Now, I'm tame as a kitten."

"Are you?" Stella challenged blithely. "I don't know that I'd call moving across the world to start a business 'tame.'"

"You would if you'd been barhopping with me when I studied for a semester in Berlin!"

Of course, that sparked a whole new series of questions from Gwen, and Stella just listened while they talked. Felicia was so worldly. She'd traveled to so many places that, sometimes, it made Stella feel a little small. The world was so vast, and she'd seen so little of it. Would her art benefit from having seen more of the world? Sometimes, she felt it might.

Before they left, after spending much longer than she'd intended at the tea house, Felicia stopped her before she could leave.

"Oh, Stella, in the excitement I almost completely

forgot!" she began. "My brother is coming into town soon, and I think you two should meet."

Stella smiled. "Of course. I would love to."

"Good!" she exclaimed. "I'm so glad. I think you two might really get on. He's funny, like you are. He's been a bit of a serial monogamist in recent years, but I think he's just looking for the right person."

Stella rolled her eyes. "I don't know about all that, but I definitely can't wait to meet him after how you speak about him. Just let me know when he's in town. We'll work something out, okay?"

"Only if you promise not to tell him the nice things I've said about him. They'll go straight to his head."

Stella laughed and they hugged good-bye. She joined Gwen in the car, hoping she hadn't overheard anything from that last part of the conversation.

As she drove, Gwen raved about how enchanting she'd found Felicia, but Stella found herself only able to half-focus on what she was saying. Her mind was wandering to what Felicia had said at the end about her brother, Graham. Maybe Stella shouldn't even meet him. If Felicia had expectations that the two of them would spark up a relationship, she was surely going to be sorely disappointed. There was no way that Stella was ready for that yet. Sure, it had been over three years since the divorce, but the circumstances were not normal. They'd been married for so long, and they had a daughter together. No one could possibly expect her heart to heal so quickly.

She supposed that didn't matter. Felicia knew that Stella was divorced, and even though it wasn't necessarily recent, Felicia would respect her for not being ready to think about getting into a new relationship just yet. It wasn't even as though Stella wasn't over Jeff. She was, or, at least, she felt like she was. She certainly had no feelings of desire toward him, no thoughts of wanting to be with him again. Missing Jeff was the last way she would describe her feelings. It wasn't that she wasn't over her last relationship. It was simply that she wasn't ready to open herself up to that kind of hurt all over again. Not to mention how Kelsey would take the prospect of her dating again.

No, she decided. She wouldn't allow Felicia to believe there was even a modicum of a chance that Stella would be interested in Graham. She would nip this in the bud before she allowed Felicia to introduce the two of them.

# Chapter Five

Stella had forgotten just how nice it was to always have family around. Gwen was never far away when they'd lived in Atlanta, especially when Kelsey was growing up. They had done everything as a family whether it was a trip to the zoo or a birthday party or a holiday. She'd been there when Kelsey had fallen off her bicycle, broken her elbow, and had to have surgery. It had been one of the worst days of Stella's life, even considering everything that would come after. She wasn't sure she would have been able to bear hearing the pained cries of her nine-year-old daughter if not for Gwen in her ear, telling stories of all the bumps and bruises Jeff had gotten playing sports growing up, reassuring her that everything would be okay.

And it was. Everything was okay for a long time. Kelsey had recovered almost the entire range of motion she'd had in her arm before the break and didn't seem to miss what she'd lost at all.

Gwen couldn't have prepared her for what happened. Reassurances felt empty, and besides, Stella didn't want to bother her mother-in-law who was dealing with so much grief of her own. Stella felt like she was the one who needed to be supporting Gwen this time, not the other way around. She still blamed herself for not being strong enough to do so.

Having Gwen around the house reminded Stella of old times. She had someone to talk to when Kelsey spent her fall break sleeping until noon. There was a reason to cook a big breakfast, now that it wasn't just the two of them eating it. It was nice not to feel alone, even though it wasn't doing anything for her productivity. She itched to paint, but this was a much-needed break. She wasn't sure when she had last taken time off, but it had been long enough, and this was welcome.

Most days, they ended up at the beach for at least an hour or so. Gwen liked it more than she had thought she would. The weather was perfect for lying in one of the large wooden reclining chairs that lined the shore, and she was content to spend the warmest part of the day lying on the sand.

The only issue Stella was encountering was that Gwen could be slightly nosy. She liked to believe that she had all the answers because she had already lived a successful life. When Stella's parents had passed, she had relied on Gwen for advice constantly. Stella hadn't been much older than Kelsey was now, and though she had thought herself all-knowing and mature at the time, the loss had made her realize just how little she did know about the world. Between her grief and the overwhelming amount of respon-sibility she suddenly had to assume, she'd nearly fallen apart. Gwen had been there to hold her hand the whole way. She'd been with her during every meeting with her lawyers, so she could accept her parents' life savings. They'd had no life insurance, given that they were barely forty when they passed, and they were both still working, so they didn't have much in the way of savings. It had been enough to support Stella until she and Jeff were married and then again when after the divorce when she'd needed to move. Only since the gallery opened had Stella been able to stop dipping into the nest egg and live solely on her own income for the first time in her life.

Gwen was opinionated. When Kelsey slept in until noon, Gwen never failed to mention that it would be better for her to keep a more regular sleep schedule. She took dishes from the dry rack and silently washed away spots that Stella hadn't noticed. Stella tried to be patient, and she'd always been good at holding her tongue, especially with people she loved. It wasn't until she found out that Gwen had overheard her conversation with Felicia about Graham that she began to feel her control slipping slightly.

"You're not really thinking about letting that woman set you up on a blind date, are you, Stella?" she asked while they were having another lunch of sandwiches on the beach. Stella hesitated, unsure of how to react.

"You mean my friend, Felicia?" she asked. The term "that woman" had thrown her off, as she had gotten the impression that Gwen had liked her.

"Yes," Gwen agreed distastefully. "That one. She mentioned something about having you meet her brother."

"Well, yes. I'm going to meet him when he comes into town, but it's not going to be in any romantic context. I've been friends with Felicia for a while, and her family rarely visits. I'm excited to meet him, just like I was excited to have you meet her. We're practically family."

Gwen huffed a sigh of irritation, clearly not convinced. "That doesn't appear to be your friend's attitude toward this."

"What does that matter?" Stella challenged. "I'm in control of my romantic life. Even if I were into the idea of blind dates, which I'm *not*, by the way, I don't feel ready. I'm still hurting after everything that happened with Jeff."

"It makes sense to still have feelings for him," Gwen agreed quickly. Her attitude had shifted rapidly, almost like she had been waiting to hear his name. "You two were married for a long time. You have a child, a beautiful one."

Stella frowned. "I didn't say I have feelings for him. I don't, Gwen. That's not on the table for us."

Gwen shook her head, almost as if she could shake off the words. "I know you're still angry, but—"

"I'm not angry. I'm really not. I'm ashamed about what happened. I feel like I have to keep all the details about my life, my marriage, and my divorce a secret from everyone I meet. It's still haunting me."

"What do you mean?"

Stella sighed. "Remember when I told you about the art exhibit that I hosted a few months ago? The one where I was originally supposed to have a partner, but she dropped out just before we could throw the event?"

"Of course I do. Adelle, right? You mentioned she had to go back to New York to be with her husband."

"That's not exactly the whole story." Stella took a steadying breath. She hadn't told Gwen much about what had happened with Adelle. She'd been afraid it would hurt her feelings to know that she was still suffering so much because of what her son had done to her. She hadn't wanted Gwen to worry, but now, it seemed as though she had to.

"What happened?"

"Her husband found out that I was Jeff's wife and decided that he couldn't be associated with criminals."

Gwen gasped. "You're not a criminal!"

"I know that," she said, "and Adelle knows that now. But her husband had this certain idea in his head about who I was, and it very nearly ended our friendship. Apparently, he felt as though his career was in danger if he were to have friends who were embezzlers."

Gwen took a long pause, seeming to collect her thoughts. "I know you've suffered as a result of what Jeff did. And I know it must be difficult to think about a future with him. But let me ask you this, Stella: Isn't it harder to imagine a future without him?"

That gave Stella pause. She really hadn't thought about that. The past three and a half years had been about finding herself and about getting her own life straightened out enough to be able to survive. When she was with Jeff, her future had been all planned out. They had already had their child, and they weren't planning on having any more. They would put Kelsey through college, and Stella would go back to work afterward to ensure that they had a comfortable savings on which to retire. Jeff was going to continue working at his company for the next decade and a half while Stella taught painting classes and sold art to make money. Things weren't perfect within their marriage. Things never were. However, they had been happy, and that had been the only thing that mattered.

When he was arrested, Stella hadn't had time to reconsider her future. She was too busy thinking about how to get through the present. Everything had fallen apart, and nothing made any sense. Her dreams of spending her retirement with her husband had fallen apart in mere moments, and it had felt like the floor had dropped out from beneath her.

The next several months had just been about getting through. Kelsey had been so upset, and the only thing Stella had wanted was to make things right within that relationship. She really hadn't even thought about Jeff in months. Every time he crossed her mind, it was in anger.

Could she picture a future without him? Had she already done so?

"None of this is the life I had planned for myself and my daughter," she said slowly. "I still find myself expecting the rest of my life to be filled with sipping tea on my balcony with my husband after we both retire. But that's not an option for me anymore."

Gwen shook her head. "It could be," she argued. "I know he hurt you, but that's what relationships are. Love is pain. What he did, he did because he thought it was the best thing for your family. I think you should think about forgiving him."

Stella couldn't form a response. She couldn't even think about that, not yet. Gwen seemed to sense this and quickly changed the subject, but the thoughts were already rolling through Stella's head and wouldn't stop. Did she really need Jeff? Did Jeff need her?

"I have to get to the studio," she said. "I'm already late to open up. Do you have any special plans for today? I won't be too long at the studio."

Gwen nodded, apparently disappointed that their conversation hadn't been more productive. She was used to people agreeing with her, and when that didn't happen immediately, she tended to take it personally.

"I've brought a few books I've been hoping to get through," she said. "I think I'm going to take one down to the beach and read for a while."

"That sounds fun," Stella said. "I'll catch up with you later. Call if you need anything."

Without giving herself a chance to argue the point further, Stella grabbed her canvas bag and took off, leaving the keys for Gwen or Kelsey and heading out the door on foot.

She felt bad ditching Gwen, and even worse, leaving her alone while Kelsey was still sleeping in the house. She could come out of her room at any moment and be roped into cheering Gwen up, but Stella really did have to open the studio. Her hours lately had been less and less, being so wrapped up in spending time with family activities, and she really needed to do some cleaning. The floors were starting to get dirty with sand tracked in on the bottoms of people's shoes.

After sweeping, Stella was just about to start mopping the floor when the doorbell jingled with the arrival of a customer.

"Are you open?" a voice called. It was a young woman,

younger than Kelsey or about the same age, certainly not looking to purchase art. Stella dusted off her smock and nodded.

"Yes, I am. Sorry, I'm just cleaning up."

The woman grinned. "It's okay! I've come by a few times this week, but you've been closed whenever I stop in."

"Sorry about that. My mother-in-law is visiting, so I've been a bit crazed. What can I do for you?"

The young woman took a card from her purse, one that Stella recognized as one of the very few business cards that she'd printed for the art exhibit a few months ago.

"My mom was here a few months back when you threw that showing, and she grabbed this card for me. I've been wanting to take painting lessons, and she said that you might be offering them. Am I too late to sign up?"

Stella hesitated. She still hadn't really made much progress with the idea of group classes. It was something that she'd thought might be fun and would certainly be a steady source of income. Adelle was the only person Stella had ever given painting lessons, and they'd been informal since the women were such close friends. She wasn't sure if she was good enough to give real lessons to strangers.

"No, no. You're not too late," she reassured. "I'm not actually running any classes just yet. I still have some details to hammer out, so if you're looking to start right away, you might want to look into a community center or something."

The young woman shook her head. "Oh, I can wait," she said. "My mom bought one of your paintings, and I really liked it. I'm not in a rush to get started on lessons anyway. This studio is on the way home from my school, so it would be convenient to take them here. Do you happen to know when you might start offering lessons?"

"I'm really not sure. I know that's not super professional, and I apologize for that."

"That's no problem!" she exclaimed. "Would it be okay if I gave you my phone number? That way, if you do decide to offer lessons, you can call me."

While Stella didn't want to make this young woman wait, she seemed determined, and Stella didn't want to let her down. She introduced herself as Rachel when she gave her phone number to Stella, who pinned it behind the cash register. Maybe it would be the push she needed to finally get things moving.

# Chapter Six

The following week, Kelsey went back to school, leaving Stella and Gwen alone for the bulk of the day. Kelsey was catching rides from friends every day, meaning that Stella no longer had to drive her to and from the campus. While she missed the bonding time that the drive had given her with her daughter, she had to admit it was convenient to not have to worry about it, particularly in the afternoons which tended to be the busiest time for the gallery.

Gwen had encouraged her to begin offering group painting lessons. After Stella had told her about the prospective student who wanted to learn from her, Gwen had been excited. She'd reassured Stella that all her doubts about her abilities to teach in a group setting were purely nerves, and that she would be an excellent teacher. Kelsey had backed her up, as well, and even helped her again to design a sign-up feature on the website she'd created for the exhibit. So far, only one person had given their email address to receive updates, but it was a start. Not to mention, she still had the phone number of the young woman who had been in last week.

She was shocked at how little effort it had actually taken to turn the lessons from a hypothetical to a reality. She'd moved everything out of her storage room at the gallery to create a large enough space to house a few students, made a few flyers, and bought some extra easels, canvases, and paints. That had been the most anxiety-inducing part since art supplies were expensive. She was still unsure whether she would so much as break even on this venture. Kelsey and Gwen had both reminded her that the only way to know for sure was to try, so she decided that this was worth a shot. Within another week, she'd had five definitive sign-ups, mostly from the flyers, which was just about as many people as she could comfortably cram into the back room studio. She'd announced that the following week would be the first class, and that after that, they would take place every Saturday morning for eight weeks. Eight classes weren't an overwhelming commit-ment, she reminded herself, but it was at least enough to make her money back from the supplies and earn a comfortable profit, too.

"What do you think I should have my new students paint first?" Stella asked the room while she, Gwen, and Kelsey were eating dinner a few nights before the first class. "Do you think a bowl of fruit is too cliche?"

Gwen laughed. "I don't know anything about art," she said, "but aren't most of your students in their twenties or younger? Maybe you should have them paint something a bit more exciting."

"What did you paint with Adelle when you started lessons with her?"

Stella grimaced slightly. "A bottle of wine," she admitted, "which we also drank. It was a pretty informal class."

Kelsey snorted. "Maybe you could have them do something like that."

"I think it's always best to start off painting an object that doesn't move. It allows you to get a feel for curves and lines, plus it's a nice introduction to shading and the direction of light and shadow."

Gwen looked impressed. "That's very technical for a painting of a wine bottle."

"There's always more to it than what's on the surface."

Kelsey slammed her fork down in excitement. "Oh, I know! What if you had everyone bring their favorite drink to paint? You have that long table to set the cans on. It would be personal for each student, plus they could drink it while they paint."

Stella grinned. "That's brilliant. I love it. I'll send out an email tonight."

When she actually got around to sending out the email, she realized that many of her students had signed up with student email addresses from Kelsey's school, meaning that they were likely people who went to the same community college. Stella remembered the flyers that Kelsey had offered to spread around the art building, which she hadn't expected to draw any attention even on the off chance that Kelsey didn't forget to put them up. Apparently, she had remembered, and they'd been surprisingly effective.

Her first class had gone off without a hitch. All her

students had brought their favorite beverages to paint. Because the students were largely so young, it was a lot of energy drinks, but the young woman whom she'd talked to in person had brought a can of iced tea with a delicate flower design on the bottle. An older woman Stella recognized from the exhibit had brought a mug and a thermos, which she'd filled with hot chocolate. It was going to take a few sessions to finish the paintings, but everyone seemed to be catching on quickly. She was excited to see what the future held for her new artists.

Gwen took Stella out to dinner after her first successful art class. Kelsey had taken a job as a teaching assistant on campus and often stayed late at school helping to grade papers and clean glass equipment for the biochemistry lab. She wasn't able to make it to dinner, but she wouldn't have liked the restaurant Gwen had chosen anyway. It was uptown, in one of the most expensive areas of the entire city. Kelsey had never been a fan of seafood, which was unfortunate now that they were living on the beach where it was always fresh. The place Gwen had decided upon was a fancy seafood restaurant.

"You really didn't have to do this," Stella said when she saw the prices on the menu. The price of a lobster was outrageous. Hadn't she read an article that said lobsters used to be prison food? "We could have celebrated at a pizza joint or something. This place is so expensive. I feel guilty."

"Oh, you have nothing to feel guilty for!" Gwen promised. "I've been wanting to try this place myself. A gentleman I met on the beach told me that their blackened tilapia is simply to die for, and you know how much I love fish. This place is going to be much fresher than anything I could order in Atlanta."

Stella sighed, supposing that she had a point. It didn't make her feel any better about ordering the most expensive piece of sea bass she'd ever had, although she had to admit that it was also the best she'd ever eaten.

"You know, I hate to bring it up," Gwen said, "but I was wondering if you'd spoken to Jeff recently."

Stella blinked in surprise. "No, I haven't spoken to him since he went to prison, Gwen."

Her eyes went wide. "Really? You've never once tried to contact him? Did he not call you?"

"He did," she admitted. "I didn't pick up."

"I can't believe that."

Stella sighed. "It's true. I didn't want to speak to him. I was so angry."

"Well, of course you were, dear, when it happened. I was angry, too. But has he never called since?"

"I told him not to."

Gwen was silent for a moment. "I raised my son well. He's made some mistakes, but his heart has always, always been in the right place. If you want my advice, I think you should give him another chance. At least an opportunity to explain himself."

Stella didn't want to tell Gwen that she had not, in fact, wanted her advice. It was something that she found painful to discuss, and there was nothing Jeff could say that would change her mind. He had made his bed, and now he was going to lie in it. Whether or not he was in prison was up to the judge that had decided his sentence, but he would never again be her husband. In her own life, he had earned himself a life sentence for what he had put her and Kelsey through."

Still, it wasn't as though she could say all that to Gwen. She had supported Stella through so much, and it wasn't as though she could tell Gwen to stop talking about her own son, right? She had a right to vent some of these feelings, and it made sense that she wanted their marriage to work out. She had always been so supportive of the two of them and had talked Stella through all the disagreements they'd ever had. Gwen was the person who taught her how to argue in a constructive way where the goal was to solve the marital problem rather than to place blame.

Unfortunately, Jeff was solely to blame in this case, and there was nothing that she could do to solve this problem. Gwen knew that, too. She may have been an optimist, but she wasn't stupid. She clearly just believed that what Jeff had done was forgivable, but Stella knew that she would never be able to bring herself to trust him again.

"Just promise me you'll think about it," Gwen offered. "I want you to try to remember the good times. You two really had some, didn't you?"

Stella nodded. "Of course we did. We have a beautiful daughter, and we were married for over twenty years. It's not as if we just fell out of love, Gwen. He betrayed me, and I can't just move on from that."

"I'm not asking you to. Just... think about it. Remember that he will never, ever make a mistake like this one again. He's serving his time. Don't you think he's been punished enough?"

Stella wanted to argue and tell her that this wasn't about punishment. Her intent wasn't to make anyone feel worse. She was just doing what she had to do to survive after such a traumatic time in her life.

Instead, she forced a smile. "I'll think about it."

Gwen seemed pleased with that answer and didn't let Stella pay any of the tab or the tip, reassuring her that this was a celebration for her and that she couldn't possibly take her money. Stella was smart enough to know when someone was trying to butter her up, but again, it wasn't worth arguing.

That night, Stella didn't intend to actually think about Jeff. In fact, she had been actively working as hard as she could to push thoughts of her ex-husband and everything he'd done as far out of her mind as possible. However, while she lay under the thin blanket she had draped over the couch, listening to a thunderstorm rumble in the distance, she found that she couldn't keep her mind from wandering.

They had had good times together. There was no doubt about that. Jeff had been the person she had run to with problems for years, basically all of her adult life. Every time something upset her, she could count on Jeff to be there, ready to help her find a solution. He wasn't always the best at just listening to her vent, but the important thing was that he was there when she was in a pinch. When he'd become the problem, she hadn't known what to do. Jeff was normally the person she turned to when something went wrong, and she had to make a big decision. He had been the one who convinced her to sell her parents' home when she'd inherited it. It had been something she wanted to do, but the guilt she'd wrestled with over selling their family home had been incapacitating. He'd reassured her that her parents would want her to do what would make her life just a little easier, as the one thing they had always wanted to do was to make sure that she never had to struggle for anything.

She scoffed, unable to keep her expressions contained even in the dark, all alone in the living room. If they could only be here to see just how difficult her life had become—the twists and turns, the ups and downs. What would they tell her to do? She barely even had them in her life for long enough to really even know what they would say in this situation. When she tried to think of her mother's voice in her ear, Gwen's was the one she heard. The only problem was that now, she was being Jeff's mother more than she was acting as her own. Stella wasn't sure that the advice Gwen was giving was actually best for her.

These thoughts, combined with the discomfort of lying on the hard couch and the volume of the storm, were enough to keep her tossing and turning late into the night.

# Chapter Seven

The next morning, Stella's alarm went off what felt like mere moments after she'd finally closed her eyes, but it was closer to a few hours. She pried her eyes open and turned off the alarm on her phone even though she knew that she had to be at the gallery early. She'd received an email from a woman who was visiting from California and wanted to take a look at the gallery, and the time they had agreed upon was early. What ended up getting Stella off the couch was the fact that she didn't want to run into Gwen that morning, not after their difficult conversation the night before. She got dressed and headed down to the gallery.

The woman from California was named Maisie Washington. She had first begun corresponding with Stella a few weeks ago after Kelsey had convinced her to upload some photos of her art onto the website Kelsey had helped her to build. Maisie had sent her a simple compliment via email, and the two had begun chatting casually. Stella didn't know much about her, just that she was very interested in art and seemed to know a lot about the subject. Stella suspected that perhaps Maisie had a studio of her own, as she spoke sometimes about her own art. Stella was interested in seeing her art. She hadn't had an artist friend her own age since Adelle, and although she loved her students, they were beginners, and it was difficult to talk to them about higher concepts. Maisie could, perhaps, fill that gap.

Maisie was on time, showing up at the door exactly one minute before 7:00, the time they'd agreed to meet. She was very tall with black hair that was tightly braided and pulled into an updo at the top of her head. She was dressed in a white dress and heels, and Stella couldn't help but think she looked more like a lawyer than an artist.

"Maisie?" she confirmed, and she broke into a wide grin.

"Stella, hi! It's so nice to finally meet you." She reached out and shook her hand, and Stella smiled. "I'm so happy to be here. It's exciting to finally see your works up close."

Stella chuckled. "Wow, thank you. That's so kind. Would you like to take a look around?"

Stella guided an enthusiastic Maisie around the gallery, showing her the paintings and answering questions about her works. She was particularly interested in the still objects rather than the scenery paintings, though she was clearly impressed with both. Maisie spent a moment with each canvas, studying the brushstrokes and the use of color in a way that made Stella feel both scrutinized and honored. This was a woman who knew what she was talking about, and if she were impressed with Stella's art, then perhaps she really was more talented than she gave herself credit for.

"This is gorgeous," she said, pointing at the painting of

Gwen's ring. "Stones are so difficult to paint, I find. I tried to paint my sister's favorite opal earrings once, and it looked horrible. I hated it so much, I ended up painting over the whole thing."

Stella laughed. "I wanted to do that a few times with this one, too," she admitted. "Thank you. The ring belongs to my ex-husband's mother."

Maisie grimaced. "Sounds like a tough relationship. I assume you painted it before the divorce?"

"Actually, no," she explained. "She's in town visiting me right now, in fact. We've always been close. She's been like a mother to me."

"I wish I could say the same about mine," Maisie said lightly. "My mother-in-law is a royal terror. If I left my husband, she'd never speak to me again, and I think she'd be glad for it."

Stella couldn't imagine having such a volatile relationship with Gwen. Just the thought of it made her want to go back home immediately and apologize for their argument the night before. But she knew that if she did that, Gwen would take it as Stella conceding her own point, and she still wasn't ready to speak with Jeff.

"Family, am I right?" she asked.

"Can't live with them, can't live without them." Maisie sighed. "You mentioned that you haven't lived here for terribly long, right? Under a year?"

Stella nodded. "Yes, we're going on one year living here in Sunrise Beach. Why do you ask?"

Maisie shifted her weight from foot to foot. "Well, forgive me if this is overstepping, but I just don't see the art game being super successful in a place like this.

Artists tend to really struggle in small communities like this one. We do best in places where there are lots of offices and businesses to purchase our work for the brownie points of having local art on the walls. I'm from a tiny town in Illinois, and when I went to college for art, everyone thought I'd lost my mind. They told me that there was no way I'd succeed and that I'd give up and start working as a secretary or something within six months."

Stella gasped. "Wow. I guess you proved them wrong, huh?"

"Oh, no, not even a little bit," she said quickly. "Sure, I sold a few paintings at the beginning, but that didn't last long. I ran out of clientele just months after I started."

"That sounds awful. What did you do?"

"I moved to California."

Stella couldn't keep her eyebrows from hitting her hairline. "Really? All the way from Illinois?"

"All the way from Illinois," Maisie confirmed. "It was all I could do to survive. I needed to do something and trying to sell my art in a tiny town wasn't going to cut it."

"Is the business better there? Have you noticed a difference?"

"It's day and night!" she replied. "I made more in my first month in Cali than I did in six in my hometown. I couldn't believe it. Not to mention, I was just a kid then. I was in my twenties. This was decades ago, obviously, but the same is still true. In California, there are always new businesses cropping up on every corner, and each one wants original artwork for their walls. Whether it's a vegan cafe or a tech startup, you can't walk into a single building that doesn't have someone's paintings on the walls or sculptures on the walkway."

Stella couldn't believe what she was hearing. Was business really that different there?

"That sounds amazing. I'm so happy that things worked out that way for you. Don't you miss your hometown?"

"Of course I do, but I couldn't have made it work if I'd stayed. I would have had to give up on my dreams if I hadn't moved."

Stella's head was spinning. This was just one person's experience, she reminded herself. Not everyone would be the same. Her own art was selling better than ever after the exhibit she'd held, and she couldn't imagine that changing any time soon. It didn't seem to be slowing down. Not to mention, she wasn't relying solely on her art sales anymore. She had her painting lessons as well. She didn't have nearly as much at stake as Maisie since she had diversified her income slightly.

"Do you like it? California, I mean."

"It's gorgeous," Maisie gushed. "Honestly, it's not terribly different from here, as far as most things go. It's hot and has beautiful beaches. If you like it here, you'd like it there. The only difference is that there are a lot of young people there. So many businesses are new, and most of the restaurants are fusions or food trucks. I didn't think that I'd like it, or at least thought I would miss my life in my small town, but I wouldn't exchange it for anything."

Stella was rarely speechless, but she wasn't sure what to say in response to what Maisie was telling her. She'd only just become used to her life here—no, more than that.

She loved it here. Her neighbors had become her friends, and her friends had become her family. Kelsey had started school and was thriving there and had made friends. After Stella had been forced to rip everything away from Kelsey, from her home to her friends, she wasn't eager to think about trying to ask her to move all over again.

Still, the idea that the success she had found here was only temporary was concerning, and it made sense. Once everyone in the city had a painting or two hanging in their home or office, how would she sell anything else? Most people bought new art for their office what, once a decade? She could throw more exhibits, as she'd made an impressive profit from that night. But at the same time, it had been a major expense, and one she couldn't risk often. Between the advertising and the catering, if she hadn't sold as much as she had, she could have easily not broken even. An event like that would certainly not work if the problem was that everyone who wanted to purchase her art had already done so.

For the first time in a long time, Stella felt that her life was happy overall even if it was still chaotic and stressful and, sometimes, a little lonely. With that said, why did she feel a pull to move to California like Maisie was advising? Was this the call of adventure or just her own overly idealistic mind running too wild?

"I love your art, Stella. It's even more beautiful in person." Maisie's voice brought her back to the present, and she shook her head to clear it.

"Thank you. That really means a lot, coming from you."

"I have to ask, Stella. I've been looking for a partner for

my own business, and I just can't get enough of you and your art. Would you ever consider moving to California?"

The question was one Stella hadn't even had a chance to really consider for herself, not to mention discussing with a person she'd only just met. She opened her mouth, hoping that the right answer would simply fall out, but found that she had to decide on an answer before she could give one.

"Oh, I really don't know," she said. "I've just barely put roots down here in Sunrise Beach."

"Exactly," Maisie said. "It's harder when your roots are in deep, but you're still so new here. What's one more move?"

Stella couldn't think of what to say. The thought of moving again was overwhelming, but she couldn't deny the appeal of the version of California that Maisie was describing.

"I would have to think about it," she said, and Maisie nodded furiously.

"There's no rush," she said. "I've got all the time in the world. You've got my number and my email, and I'm in town for a bit longer. You take all the time you need. Just consider it, okay? And I'm going to send you some pictures of my favorite spots in West Covina. If that doesn't convince you to move, nothing will."

Stella smiled. "I look forward to it," she said. As she said good-bye to Maisie, Stella tried to think rationally, to remind herself that this was just her excitement getting into her head. The idea of her art career taking off was tantalizing, sure, but she couldn't think seriously about it... could she? It wouldn't be the craziest thing she'd ever done, and perhaps Kelsey wouldn't be angry about the idea, either. When they'd first arrived here, Kelsey's biggest complaint had been the lack of anything to do in town. In a big city in California, there would never be any lack of activity for her to get herself involved in. There might even be more community colleges for her to look at. She'd wanted to minor in calculus, and the small school she was attending didn't offer such a thing.

It was too much too fast, she told herself. This was just a daydream, nothing more.

Still, it couldn't hurt to look at Maisie's pictures, right?

# Chapter Eight

Two days after the conversation with Maisie, Stella had patched things up with Gwen.

Well, perhaps "patched things up" was a bit of an overstatement. She and Gwen had decided not to talk about the conversation they'd had about Jeff that had been so difficult for the both of them. It was better, in Stella's opinion, to just agree to disagree on the subject. She didn't want to make Gwen think negatively about Jeff, not at all. Even if Stella couldn't forgive him for what he'd done, she didn't want to cause a rift in their relationship. Gwen deserved to have her son in her life and, despite Stella's anger with him, Jeff deserved to have his mother in his life, too. Stella knew that she would give anything to have her own parents back in her life. She would sacrifice everything she had for one more conversation with her mother, and she didn't want to take that away from Jeff, no matter how much she might hate him.

As she sat in her new studio attached to the gallery and

painted the scene she saw out the window, the cloudy sky with the city on the horizon, she wondered if she really did hate Jeff or if that was just what she liked to tell herself.

The cloudy but sunny sky didn't hold her attention the same way that storms tended to. Thunder and lightning were a much more compelling subject to capture, and although she thought the city was beautiful, it wasn't the most exciting. Her mind wandered, and there were more than enough topics for her thoughts to drift to.

The most pressing, of course, and what she expected to be unable to drive from the forefront of her mind was what Maisie had said about California, but that wasn't what she found herself obsessing over.

Instead, she was thinking, not for the first time since the divorce, about her ex-husband.

Gwen had made her promise to think about the good times. The promise had been hollow in the moment, but now, she was unable to stop thinking about them.

She thought about their first date. Jeff had asked her to their high school homecoming dance, and she'd been so excited to say yes. Jeff was something of a heartthrob in their high school, and Stella hadn't thought that she would ever have a chance with a boy like him. She was active in the theater club, painting the sets for the school plays and musicals. The crowd she ran with tended to be a little nerdier, even if that word was a little harsher than what she would have used to describe herself at the time.

Stella had always been beautiful, there was no doubt about that. Perhaps that was what had gotten the attention of the star of the baseball team, Jeff Britton. If it wasn't her beauty, it might have been the fact that she was a straight A student while Jeff struggled in English class. That was the reason he'd talked to her in the first place. The class had to read *Wuthering Heights*, one of Stella's favorite books, and Jeff was struggling to get through the book at all. They'd had an essay due, and Jeff just had no idea where to start. She had felt him tap on her shoulder, she had turned around so that her long, brown ponytail was out of her face, and the rest was history. She'd helped him to get an A on the essay through lots of late nights in the library, many of which had ended in kissing, and he'd asked her to the homecoming dance.

That memory was one she hadn't thought about in years, much longer than even the beginning of the divorce. Some things just get lost to time, she thought, and those happy childhood moments were often some of the first things to go, especially considering that not even a year later, Stella's parents passed away. That tended to be the only thing she thought of when she tried to recall that time of her life—her senior year of high school.

Good times had been few and far between for a while after that, but gradually, laughter had begun to have a place in Stella's life again, and most of the time, Jeff was the person behind it. He always knew just what to say to make her smile, even when she didn't want to. Jeff was silly. He made jokes, dumb ones, which never failed to make her giggle, even if she was rolling her eyes at the same time.

Even though she was remembering something that was so sweet and dear to her heart, Stella couldn't help but feel mixed emotions about the memory. A smile was playing at her lips, but her eyes were filled with tears.

Stella decided that was enough painting and thinking

for one evening and cleaned up her paints. It was getting close to dinner time anyway, and Kelsey and Gwen would want her home to eat. She took care to close up her shop and lock the doors before heading back home.

Kelsey and Gwen were sitting in the living room playing chess. Kelsey had never been much of a fan of board games, but she looked like she was enjoying this one. She supposed that they hadn't heard her come in through the back door, as she could hear their conversation, just light chatter, going on until she entered the room. As soon as she appeared in the doorway, Kelsey stood to leave.

"Kelsey," Gwen complained, "what about our game? Don't you want to finish?"

She shook her head, pointedly ignoring her mother. "We will later," she said. "I have homework."

It was likely true, but it was still a lame excuse. Stella knew exactly why she was really leaving.

"What was that all about?" Gwen, less clued into the situation, asked. Stella rolled her eyes.

"She's mad at me for something or other," she said. She was used to this. It had been a relatively common occurrence since Kelsey turned thirteen. She would find something to be angry about, anything from Stella finishing the last yogurt to not allowing her to hang out with her friends on a school night. She would ice Stella out without so much as a word about why she was angry until Stella buttered her up with pizza. That was usually the only way to get Kelsey to talk when she was angry. Sometimes, Stella believed Kelsey picked fights just because she had a craving for pizza. She was trying not to take it too personally.

"What happened? Did the two of you fight?"

Stella shook her head. "Nothing dramatic like that," she said, setting down her bag and pouring herself a tall glass of iced tea. The walk home had been hot, and Gwen had filled the refrigerator with the stuff. Stella had never been able to make it as sweet as Gwen could. It was some Georgia secret, she supposed.

"Well, what's she so angry about then?"

"I don't know," she admitted. "I'm sure she'll tell me sooner or later. It's not a good idea to pry with Kelsey. She has to decide to come around on her own. If you try to make her talk to you before she's ready, it usually backfires. Trust me."

Gwen didn't look convinced, but she didn't argue. "If you're sure," she said. "How was the rest of your day? Did you finish the painting you said you wanted to make?"

"Not just yet," Stella said. "There's something off about it, and I can't put my finger on it. I think the weather has just been so beautiful lately, and it's been so hot. The sky is too pretty to be interesting, and all the flowers and animals are hiding from the sun."

Gwen didn't look like that made a lot of sense to her, but Stella hadn't expected it to. She supposed that a lot of people would rather have a painting of a clear and sunny sky than an overcast one anyway, and she'd painted a lot of them in the past. Perhaps the sky wasn't the real reason she was struggling to focus.

"I have a question for you," Gwen asked suddenly. Stella braced herself for yet another conversation she didn't want to have.

"Okay," she said. "Why do I feel like you're not going to ask me what I want for dinner?"

Gwen was not swayed by her attempt to lighten the mood and frowned. "I'm being serious. I don't mean to pry, and I don't want to push you away. I really don't want our relationship to suffer as a result of this, Stella, I hope you believe me on that."

Stella nodded. "I do." She did. Gwen most likely believed that she was doing her a favor.

"Good. I want to know if you've contacted Jeff since we last spoke. Since I told you to remember the good times and to think about it."

Stella shook her head and sighed. "No, I haven't. I told you, I'm not planning on doing that. We're finished. I don't wish him ill or anything, but I don't have any desire to speak to him ever again. That's just the honest truth. I'm sorry." The only part of what she'd said that wasn't true was the fact that she was sorry. Really, this was her own personal business and none of Gwen's, even if it did involve her son. Stella's marriage, or the memory of it, was her own, and Gwen didn't have a part of that.

"I just think that time heals all wounds, honey. If you were to talk to him, I think you might find that things would go back to being like they were a bit easier than you would think."

Stella couldn't believe what she was hearing. Her mother-in-law had always been a bit of a meddler but never to this extent. Stella had always thought that there were boundaries, and until now, Gwen had always been good about accepting that problems within their marriage were for the couple to deal with privately. She would never have guessed that Gwen might be this pushy about the subject.

"I don't want things to go back to how they were," she reminded Gwen. "Don't you remember how things were just before we separated? They weren't exactly sunshine and roses."

If she were being honest, part of the reason she didn't want to talk to Jeff was because of the fact that they might be tempted to fall back into old routines. She might laugh at his jokes, and that might lead to remembering what a great dad he had always been to Kelsey, which might lead to hearing him out about the choices he'd made that had torn their family apart. She didn't want to forgive him. Even if she did, that wasn't what was best for their family, especially for Kelsey. Kelsey deserved stability, and Stella had told her that she and Jeff were getting a divorce. She couldn't possibly go back on what she'd said and under-mine Kelsey's trust just because she still had stale feelings of love for her ex-husband in her heart. She'd only just accepted the divorce, and Stella wasn't about to undo all that emotional work by telling Kelsey that she was going to speak with Jeff again.

"I just want you to think about what's best for you and your family," Gwen persuaded. Stella tried her best to keep the rising anger and irritation down. "Families are happier together."

"Jeff is behind bars, Gwen. What kind of togetherness would that even be?"

"He's not there forever, sweetheart. He's going to get out before you know it. Don't you want someone to grow old with? You planned out a whole future together. I'm just surprised you're willing to give it all up."

Stella took a soothing deep breath before she answered. Yes, she had built a whole future with Jeff. She'd thought that her life after Kelsey moved out would be her and Jeff growing old together, keeping one another safe and warm and loved.

Now, she had to find those things on her own. She had to find them in other places, sources that weren't her husband. And she'd been doing a good job of it so far, if she did say so herself. She had made friends, ones that gave her love and support and advice. Even if things weren't always easy, and she certainly still had lonely nights, she wouldn't trade her life here for anything. The people who cared for her here were too important to her to give up on what she'd made for herself.

"I'm not giving up," she replied. "I'm just choosing something different. I loved what I had with Jeff, but he made it clear that wasn't an option anymore. I had to start over, and Kelsey and I are only just starting to get really comfortable here. And I think that's the end of this discussion."

Gwen nodded, though Stella had a feeling she was accepting the fact that the conversation was over more than she was accepting what Stella had said. She began to pick up the chess game that she and Kelsey hadn't finished. Neither of them felt like playing anymore, she supposed.

Great. Now everyone in her house was angry with her.

Stella tried to push it from her mind as she went to the kitchen to cook the dinner that she knew everyone would eat in separate rooms of the house to avoid her. The one thing she knew for sure was that she was happy with what she was doing and where she was living, and nothing was going to change that. She could only hope that Gwen wasn't talking to Kelsey about these same issues and giving her false hope that she and Jeff would work things out, or worse, blaming her for the fact that they weren't going to.

# Chapter Nine

The next morning, though Stella had told herself that she was intending to call Maisie and tell her that she wasn't interested in moving to California, she ended up not doing so. After all, it was Saturday, and she was teaching an early class. She didn't want to call and wake Maisie just to pass along a message that could be delivered at any time. She decided she would do that later and headed down to her studio to get everything ready for her students.

Stella loved to prepare the space for her students. She found it almost therapeutic, and it always made her so excited for the class ahead. First, she swept the floor, ensuring that any sand that anyone had tracked into the gallery was cleaned up. Next, she began to set out the stools for everyone to sit on. She'd bought a few nice wooden stools along with the easels, which she set up next in front of each seat, from a local furniture store. The owner had done her a favor and ordered the easels specially for her, as they weren't something they normally sold. Stella had bought several, never in a million years expecting that she would use them all at once. Once the furniture was set up, she moved on to the paints. That was the part that excited her most, as she loved to think about what the students might create with them that day.

At first, her classes had been fairly rigidly structured. She would tell the students what to paint at the beginning of class and give them pointers along the way. Now, though, things were a little more relaxed since her students had the hang of the fundamentals. Rather than telling them what to paint, she would give them a broad topic like a landscape or a still object. Each class was still meant to focus on something specific, whether it was movement or lighting or color theory, but everyone had a little bit more freedom to choose what they actually wanted to paint. It meant that they were always much happier with the final product because it meant something to them.

She was really impressed with how they were coming along, too. Each person had their own agenda, the thing that they were trying to get out of her class, and she felt honored to be able to guide them toward their goals and watch how much easier it was for them to put the images in their heads onto paper.

Most of the time, they were doing landscape work, as that was Stella's specialty and what most of her students had mentioned they wanted to work up to painting. She was constantly impressed with the scenes they could come up with. There was a lot of creativity in the group, and it was fun to see them unlocking it.

The money wasn't half bad, either. Stella was making more overall charging by the hour than she had been selling her art, and it was much more consistent. For the first time in a long time, she had a regular paycheck—one she could depend upon, and that was a good feeling. She knew that she was definitely independent from Jeff and from the money that her parents had left her when they'd passed away. She could focus on saving and even think about expanding her business. Should she offer more classes? Right now, she only had one per week, but she supposed that it couldn't hurt to teach a few more if there was enough interest in them.

Speaking of selling her paintings, that part of her business was still going quite well. At least a few times a month, people came in and bought a painting or two. It didn't sound like much, and sometimes Stella felt a little anxious with all the time she felt she spent just sweeping and painting. But because the paintings always sold for so much, it was a considerable amount of income. All in all, things were going well, and, even though Stella had occupied most of the past three years with worrying about the future, she felt confident rather than concerned.

The next day, Stella decided to head back over to the other side of town to visit Felicia again. She had thought about bringing Gwen, but honestly, she didn't really want to. Gwen had been so judgmental when Felicia had brought up her brother, who Stella assumed was still going to be coming to town relatively soon, and it had made both of them feel uncomfortable. Not to mention, Felicia was a very headstrong and stubborn person. If she were committed to having Graham meet Stella, there was nothing that anyone could say to change her mind.

With that in mind, Stella made the choice to tell Gwen that she was heading up to the gallery. Instead, she visited with Felicia uptown. What Gwen didn't know wouldn't hurt her, and besides, she and Kelsey were probably having a grand time saying passive aggressive things about her behind her back. Gwen was one of those people who liked to air out dirty laundry to anyone who would listen, and Stella still hadn't figured out why Kelsey was so upset with her.

A cup of tea and a sandwich would get her mind off all of that, she thought. She needed it now more than ever.

Stella was sure that Felicia had a sixth sense about when she came through the door. Perhaps it was just a security camera. All she knew was that by the time she'd parked her car, Felicia was already rushing to the front of the store to greet her.

"Stella!" she greeted excitedly. "I've got your order already put in with the chef, my darling. How have you been?"

Stella grinned, allowing her cheeks to be kissed in Felicia's typical, friendly manner. "It's been a week," she admitted. "I could use a cup of calming tea." She followed Felicia to the corner booth and sat down beside her.

"Is it your mother-in-law?" she asked, and Stella rolled her eyes.

"And my daughter," she said. Felicia grimaced. "Yeah. It's not a great time in my house right now."

"Well, what happened?"

"Which one?"

"Start with Kelsey."

Stella shrugged. "Honestly, I don't even know. I think it

might have something to do with the fact that a bunch of her friends are taking my art class. I'm not sure if she's upset that they're busy on Saturdays now, or what, but I think that's what's making her so mad."

"That sounds difficult. What are you going to do?"

"What can I do?" she asked. "It's not like I can just kick her friends out of class, you know? They paid, and they have a right to be there if they like it. I'm not going to turn away business for Kelsey's social life. She can live without a few Saturday mornings with her friends."

"Tough love," Felicia teased. "I like it. You're always so soft for her, it's nice to see this side."

"I'm not soft!"

"Oh, she has you in the palm of her hand." Felicia scoffed, and Stella knew that it was true, as much as she didn't want to admit it. She would do anything for Kelsey, no matter how inconvenient. Still, she couldn't fire students just because Kelsey was feeling lonely.

"Yeah, yeah." She laughed. "Well, she's not the only problem."

"Right. Gwen. What's going on with her? She seemed perfectly lovely when I met her last week."

Stella nodded. "She is, but she's also the type of person where you don't want to be on her bad side."

"And you've made the list?"

"I'm not sure yet," she said, pausing to thank the waiter as he brought their teas and lunches. "She keeps talking to me about getting back together with my ex-husband."

Felicia nodded. "I hate to say I saw that coming, love, but—"

"I know," Stella interjected. "I probably should have,

but I thought we had a more solid relationship than that. I told you my parents died when I was in high school. Gwen was practically like a mother to me. I owe her so much, and I love her outside of my relationship with Jeff. I was really hoping that I wouldn't have to lose that."

Felicia looked empathetic but not optimistic. "Do you really think you can, though? I mean, it seems like a tall order to ask her not to think about her own son's best interests. Which are *clearly* to be with you, as you are charming in every way."

Stella laughed and rolled her eyes. "Thank you," she said. "But I don't know. I'm not ready to give up on it yet. I still need her in my life, you know?"

"Well, if you want some good news, Graham's flight is booked. He's departing tomorrow from Manchester Airport."

"Ooh, I imagine that's a long flight."

"It is, a bit," she admitted, "but I've made it for the past several holidays, and it's his turn to do it."

"Are you excited to see him?"

"Beyond excited!" she grinned. "I'm chuffed. I can't wait. I hope you two will get on like I think you will."

Stella still didn't have any interest in meeting Graham with any sort of romantic intentions, but she was looking forward to meeting him. Stella had been an only child and so had Jeff, so she had very few sibling figures in her life. Part of her was hoping that perhaps Graham would see his little sister's best friend as sort of a sister, too, and that they could grow to be good friends. The way Felicia described him, he was funny, kind, and smart, just like Felicia herself.

The two were so close, Stella was curious about what kind of a person he might be.

"We'll have lunch or something once he settles in—all of us," she said. Felicia had met Gwen, of course, and she'd also met Kelsey a few times. Stella had brought Kelsey here to the tea house twice, but she wasn't much of a tea person. Felicia had also come to the house to watch movies and drink wine with Stella on more than one occasion since they'd met, and Kelsey had been around some of those times. Kelsey liked her, even if she didn't know her well, and Stella was sure that Gwen would be happier with Stella meeting Graham if it were a big family affair. On the other hand, she didn't want to overwhelm him by showing up with her whole family, so she supposed that they would have to play that part by ear.

The women finished their lunches, chatting about their plans for the week and what little gossip either of them knew. Felicia always had something interesting to say about her employees, so much so that it made Stella a little grateful that she was able to run her gallery by herself and didn't need to hire help.

She was still a little nervous about meeting Graham, knowing that Felicia had certain expectations that were clear even though she swore that she understood Stella wasn't looking for a new partner. However, there was certainly no harm in just meeting someone, right? All she had to do was shake the man's hand and have lunch with him. It wasn't a blind date. This could be friendly and casual if she let it be, so she tried to keep her nerves away from her mind and focus on being excited to meet her new friend's closest family member.

# Chapter Ten

Stella continued to try contacting Maisie over the next few days, but she was finding her elusive. She had tried calling, texting, and even emailing, but none of that had worked for the first three days of reaching out.

On Saturday morning, while Stella was setting up everything for her students, the doorbell to the gallery rang. Stella came out from the studio in the back room and felt relief wash over her when her eyes met Maisie's.

"Hey, Maisie," she greeted. "I'm so sorry. I've been trying to get ahold of you."

"I know," Maisie replied. "I got your messages. I wanted to stop by before I left anyway, so I figured I'd just wait until I saw you in person."

"Well, I hate to be the bearer of bad news, but I'm afraid I don't have the answer you want."

Maisie looked a little disappointed but not surprised. "I figured," she admitted. "I'm guessing you're saying you don't want to consider moving to California?"

"I did consider it," Stella reassured. "I really did. It's

just not where I am in my life right now. I like where I'm living, and I don't want to change everything up just yet."

"That's a shame, but I can't say I'm surprised. I knew it was a long shot."

"I'm sorry. I know it's not what you wanted."

"It's okay!" Maisie chirped. "Hey, I'm going to run another idea by you, and you don't have to say yes, but I'd like you to think about it. What if you stayed in Sunrise Beach, and I sold your paintings out in California?"

"Like a consignment sort of a deal?"

"Exactly!"

Stella paused. She hadn't thought about that before, but now that the opportunity was on the table in front of her, it seemed sort of appealing. She'd been opposed to selling to that man who had wanted to buy her gallery, Max Carson, but that had been a different scenario. He had offered to buy her out completely and commission her, selling only the art that she painted explicitly for him. It had meant sacrificing her creative freedom to paint whatever Max wanted her to paint. This would be someone selling her existing paintings, ones she painted because she wanted to, and taking a cut of the profits for having done the footwork of the sale. Maisie would be spreading her name to California's art community which was something Stella had to admit she liked the sound of.

"You know, that actually sounds like it could work," she said. "I like that idea."

"Really? That's amazing!" Maisie exclaimed. "I'm in town for a few more days, so I'll stop by sometime to pick up a few paintings. Then we'll talk about how this will work and how we'll get the paintings to me in the future, so

I don't have to come back every time. I know it sounds like a lot, but I have a feeling your paintings are going to sell pretty well, so I want to make sure we're prepared."

"That sounds perfect, Maisie. Just let me know before you plan to come in, and I'll make sure I'm here."

The two said their good-byes, and Stella sat for a long moment before remembering that she didn't have time to dwell on how she was feeling. Her art students would be in soon, and she had to be ready to teach.

After Stella finished teaching, she decided she would close up the gallery for the day after everyone left. Saturdays were one of her busier days for selling artwork, sure, but she was feeling exhausted and not up to standing around and waiting for people who may or may not even show up. With all the stress of Gwen and Kelsey being so angry with her, she hadn't slept well. Not to mention, sleeping on the couch was beginning to take its toll on her back.

She had taken the car to the studio since she had some art supplies to restock and hadn't been able to carry them all in a bag. But now that she was there, she regretted it a bit. She felt as though she could use the walk to sort through her thoughts. As much as she wanted to tell someone about the deal she'd just made, she didn't think that anyone in her home at the moment was in the mood to feel particularly celebratory for her success. She knew that this was probably something she'd have to text Felicia about later. Kelsey would come around, she was sure. She always did.

Gwen was a different story entirely. In all her years of

knowing Gwen, she'd only been upset with her like this a handful of times. Once had been after a bad fight when Stella had first become pregnant with Kelsey. Some unpleasant combination of hormones, constant nausea, and aching feet had made Stella moodier than she'd ever been, and she knew it, even at the time. She'd secluded herself to her and Jeff's bedroom since it was the one with a bathroom attached, and she was still unable to hold down much of anything. Anyone who came to check on her was in the line of fire, and Jeff had been so worried about her getting dehydrated or feeling dizzy and falling that he'd called his mother over to look after her.

Of course, Gwen had accepted. There were few things she loved more than doting on someone who needed it, and she'd been almost more excited than the couple themselves about the pregnancy. She'd wanted to be a grandmother since Jeff had first married, and she was finally getting her wish.

The problem was that Stella wasn't exactly the most pleasant sick person to be around. She was notoriously venomous toward anyone who tried to chat with her when she didn't feel well, and Jeff had neglected to tell Gwen. He'd figured that, because the relationship between Stella and Gwen was so strong, she would be spared from the line of fire.

He'd been wrong.

Just a few days into being looked after, Stella had snapped at Gwen badly. Stella had been irritable since the beginning, but Gwen had been willing to let the small things roll off her shoulders. Stella couldn't even remember what she'd said, now. Something about leaving her alone, probably, but her words had been unkind. She may have even cursed. She regretted it immediately, of course, but the damage had been done. For the remainder of the week, Gwen hadn't spoken to her at all. She'd ignored all of Stella's attempts at an apology, bringing her water and soup broth and holding her hair back while she was sick in silence. Taking care of her had still been Gwen's priority, even as angry as she was, Stella thought.

That time, it had taken a lot to make Gwen forgive her. Stella had cried, saying that she had no idea why she was feeling so moody and angry, and Gwen had finally taken pity on her.

"It's okay, darling, it's okay," she'd reassured, rushing to sit beside her on the bed and rubbing circles on her back. "These things are hard, and you've been so ill. I understand. Just try to remember that I'm here for you, okay? Jeff and I are just doing our best."

Stella had shaped up considerably after that. Though the mood swings had taken a few more weeks to wear off, she'd gotten better at holding her tongue, and that seemed to be enough for Gwen to forgive her.

Stella had no idea what she was going to do this time. She didn't think she had it in her to break down crying again, and besides, even if she could, it would be disingenuous. Of course, she was sad that Gwen wasn't speaking to her, but she didn't feel the same way she had about the argument they'd had when she was pregnant.

During that fight, she'd been in the wrong. When she'd finally come out on the other side of the hormonal, sleep-deprived anger, she'd felt terrible for how she had treated her mother-in-law who was only trying to care for her even if it was a little suffocating at times. This time, however, Stella didn't feel that she was in the wrong.

If she were being honest, she felt that Gwen should stop pushing so hard. This issue was none of her business, even if it did involve her son. She wasn't sure how a woman as stubborn as Gwen would find a way to forgive her if Stella weren't sobbing and exclaiming that the whole disagreement was all her fault.

"Mrs. Britton?" a voice pulled her from her thoughts, and she turned around to see two of her students that she recognized to be Kelsey's friends. They were art students who had helped her with the flyers from her exhibit a few months ago. The short girl was named Dani, and the boy next to her was Joey. Stella was pretty sure they'd tried dating in the past, when she'd first started teaching her class, but she thought they'd called it off and gone back to just being friends. They stopped carpooling and holding hands but still seemed to be on good terms.

She smiled. "Oh, please, call me Stella," she said. She was a little surprised that they didn't appear to know that she wasn't "Mrs. Britton" anymore. Had Kelsey not told them about the divorce, or did they just not think about it?

"Oh, okay!" Dani said, her face brightening into a wide grin. She was cute, Stella thought, with her black dreadlocks pulled into a bun. Stella knew that this was one of Kelsey's closer friends, as she recognized her from having picked Kelsey up in her car several times on their way to study groups and fun activities. Stella waited for Dani to say something else, but neither her nor the taller boy standing beside her said a word, so Stella smiled.

"What can I do for you two?"

"We were just wondering if we could ask you some questions," Joey said. Stella nodded.

"Of course. Anything. What do you want to know?"

"Well, I don't know if your daughter ever talks about us," Dani said, "but we're both traditional art students. Traditional as in not graphic design or digital art."

"That's a bold choice in this day and age," Stella said. "I'm impressed. You're both very good."

"Aw, thank you!" Dani chirped. "I mean, you're probably wondering why we're taking an extra class if we're studying art in school, right?"

"Sure."

Joey sighed. "It's because our school caters to the digital students way more than they care about us. The ones that want to draw with charcoal and paint with oil pastels get barely any budget and have so few classes to choose from. Our professors barely care, too. We came to your gallery and loved it, so when Kelsey told us that you were offering classes, we really wanted to take them. With you."

Stella almost blushed. "That's so sweet," she said. "Thank you. That means a lot to me."

"We should be thanking you! Our question is, I guess, are we making a big mistake choosing this career path?"

Stella blinked in surprise, not having expected the conversation to go this way. "A mistake in what way?"

"I'm sorry, I don't mean to be rude! That was super rude."

"I think what Dani means," Joey amended pointedly, and Stella could tell that they had definitely dated in the past, "is that everyone is always telling us that we're choosing a bad career path. Everyone always tells me that I should be going into math or science or something because art is so competitive, and that I'm never going to find a job."

"Same for me," Dani agreed. "My parents are always on my case about it. My dad has even threatened to stop helping me pay off my student loans if I don't go into law. He's a lawyer."

"I gathered." Stella laughed. "Well, I'm sorry you're having problems with feeling like people aren't believing in you. You're so talented, both of you, and you should feel supported by your parents and peers while you're following your dreams."

"Is it super hard, though?" Joey asked. "To make it, I mean. Is it, like, impossible to make a living?"

Stella hesitated at that, as she honestly wasn't quite sure of the answer. She'd been painting for years and hadn't made a single sale. Until recently, the idea of her art being a career hadn't even occurred to her. She'd gone to a few community art shows in Atlanta and rented a booth where she'd sold one or two paintings if she was lucky that year, but nothing exceptional. If she'd needed income, that definitely couldn't have been it. For those years, she'd made maybe a few hundred dollars a year with her art, and if she hadn't been married to a breadwinner, she probably would have had to teach instead.

Even now, she was teaching. She was doing it because she liked it, and because there was demand, but that factored into her answer, too. If neither of these students wanted to go on to be teachers, they might struggle just as she had when she'd first moved to Sunrise Beach.

Then, she thought of Maisie, and, less favorably, of Max.

Max had offered to buy her out completely just weeks after she'd opened her gallery. Of course, she'd said no, as it would have meant giving up her creative freedom to paint whatever he thought would sell, but still, working for commission like that would have been a viable way of making money if she hadn't wanted to teach. Then there was Maisie, who was going to sell her paintings on consignment in a different state, meaning that she would take a loss on the overall price of the paintings for the convenience of not having to do the legwork to sell them. The problem with opening a gallery like this in a small town was the fact that not very many new people were strolling in to see and potentially purchase her art, but in a bigger city, maybe that wouldn't be such a problem.

Stella had to ultimately resign to the fact that she didn't know for sure. She'd been lucky, at least when it came to her art career, and it didn't feel fair to give advice to someone when all she'd done was be at the right place at the right time.

"I think," she finally said, "that it's never a waste of time to do what you love. You might have to be open to some alternative ways of making money, like commissions. Does that sound like something you'd be open to, either of you?"

Both nodded. "Definitely!" said Dani. "I think that would be super fun. I've already done a few commissions for my uncle who owns a deli and wanted me to paint the menu. I really liked that."

"It wouldn't bother me, either," said Joey.

Stella nodded. "That's good. I'm not going to lie to you and say it's always been easy. I'm teaching classes, and even though I really like that, I'm not sure if I would be making consistent income if I didn't. There are always a lot of unknowns, but I don't think it's worth giving up on something you love just because people are telling you it might be hard. You already know it's going to be hard, right? And you're choosing it anyway."

Dani looked almost like she could cry. "Thank you, Stella. I really needed to hear someone say that. My mom would never believe in me like this."

Stella felt pain in her heart for this girl, no older than her daughter, barely older than she had been herself when she had lost her own mother. Joey looked moved, too, like he had needed to hear her words just as much as Dani had.

"Look, both of you are clearly talented. I think you'll be fine if you work hard and don't let anyone tell you that you have to give up if it's not what you want to do. And I'm always here for you if you need someone to talk to about these things, okay? I'm not the best at giving advice, but I care about both of you, and I want to see you both succeed."

Dani surprised her by swooping in for a hug, which Stella returned without hesitation. It felt natural, like embracing her own daughter.

Felicia was right, she thought. She had gone soft.

Oh, well. If that was what these kids needed, then she was glad for it.

Dani and Joey chatted for a few more minutes as Stella packed up the mess from the class. They helped her to clean paint brushes and put the caps on all the paints that some of the other students tended to leave open despite Stella reminding them repeatedly that they'll dry up if not handled properly. She felt a little guilty about charging

Dani and Joey money for the class if they were going to stick around and help clean up, but she couldn't seem to get rid of them. Besides, it was nice to have a helping hand. If they decided that they wanted to come back when she offered another term of classes, she would give them both a discount. She was already thinking about offering levels of classes like intermediate and advanced painting for those who had already taken the first class and wanted to go even further with their art.

Once everything was finally cleaned up and her studio was ready to open the next day, Stella turned back to the kids, who at this point, had sacrificed almost an hour of their time just to help her.

"Thank you both so much for helping me clean up," she said. "You really didn't have to do that."

Joey shook his head. "It was our pleasure. You're really fun to talk to, and you know so much about art. Our professors haven't worked as artists, you know? They all went straight to teaching, so when we have questions like this, they don't really have much advice. It's really helpful to talk to you."

Stella felt her heart squeeze again, and she sighed. "Can I buy you two lunch? As a payment for everything you've done for me today."

"Oh, you don't have to!" Dani reassured. "We did it because we wanted to."

"And I want to repay you," Stella said. If there was one thing she knew college-aged kids couldn't resist, it was a free meal. She didn't exactly have to twist their arms to get them to allow her to buy them each a sandwich from her favorite food truck near the studio on the beach. As they ate, they talked about art in a way that Stella hadn't really been able to since Adelle had moved. Maisie had been a fun person to chat with about it, but she was leaving, and she knew much more about the business side of things than the creative. These two were young and excitable and so creative. Stella found their energy to be fun even if it did make her feel a little old.

Dani and Joey thanked Stella again when lunch was done, and she headed home. As she pulled into the driveway, she realized just how much later in the day it was than the time that she had said that she'd be home. She glanced down at her phone, expecting a panicked mess of missed texts and calls from Gwen and Kelsey wondering where she was, but she had no such messages. Not even a single text wondering if she was all right or when she'd be home.

They really must be angry with her, she thought. Perhaps this wasn't something that a pizza dinner and a few days of tiptoeing around her mother-in-law was going to fix. She might really need to do some damage control.

Just to be on the safe side, she ordered the pizza ahead of time, so it would arrive for dinner. She ordered pineapple and ham on half, a concoction that she thought tasted vile, but Kelsey loved, and pepperoni and onions for herself and Gwen. Hopefully, that would at least soften the two of them enough that she could get her foot in the door to talk to them.

# Chapter Eleven

When Stella arrived home, Kelsey was in her room. Gwen was out of the house and had left a note explaining that she had walked down to the beach for some sun. Stella could tell that was likely code for "I didn't want to be home when you came inside." Oh, well, she thought. Jeff had always told her that his mother held grudges and often needed time to cool down after an argument, but Stella had never really had to test that firsthand. Whenever she and Jeff had argued, Gwen had usually been on her side.

"You know the saying," Gwen had always told him. "Happy wife, happy life." Stella had always known that she was showing favoritism toward her in a way that was biased from how unfairly Gwen had been treated in her own marriage. Her own husband had always been away, and when he was home, he nitpicked everything Gwen did. She was left to raise Jeff by herself, clean the house, do all the shopping, and all she ever heard (at least, the way Gwen told the story) was how she should have done better. Stella couldn't imagine. She and Jeff had rarely argued, but when they had, it was always resolved fairly quickly and almost never resulted in hard feelings for more than a day or so.

Arguing with her daughter, on the other hand, was a much more difficult thing to do. Kelsey was not a confrontational person though she was by no means timid. She would make her distress and upset feelings known, but she never wanted to talk about it directly. Stella supposed it was a product of her age. Eighteen-year-olds tended to prefer stomping around the house and slamming doors over having an open and honest, if difficult, conversation to resolve issues.

Stella decided that she wasn't going to play that game this time. She knocked on Kelsey's bedroom door, hoping to take advantage of Gwen's absence, and waited for an answer that didn't come.

"Kelsey," she called. She heard the soft rock music that Kelsey was listening to increase in volume to drown out her mother's calls, and she rolled her eyes. "Kels, come on. I want to talk to you."

"Go away," Kelsey commanded. "I'm doing homework."

"Well, take a break," Stella said. "I'm coming in." She didn't wait for an answer as she pushed Kelsey's bedroom door open, ignoring the indignant shout.

"Mom!" Kelsey screeched. "I said go away!"

"I heard you," Stella said, "and I will after you talk to me." Kelsey huffed.

"I have a test tomorrow. I'm busy."

"Then you'd better talk fast, huh?"

Kelsey scowled, reaching for the knob on her radio, but

Stella was faster. She pressed the power button to turn it off, so Kelsey had no choice but to listen.

"What's going on with you?"

Kelsey rolled her eyes. "Nothing. I'm fine."

Stella felt a little reassured by the fact that Kelsey seemed to mean that, but she wasn't backing down. "You're angry with me. I don't know what I did, but I want to. Talk to me, please. Why are you so upset?"

Kelsey hesitated, curling into herself for a moment. She tucked her knees up to her chest and sighed. For a long moment, Stella didn't think that she was going to speak, but Kelsey surprised her.

"Joey and Dani are, like, my two best friends."

Stella nodded. "Okay...?"

"And they're both in your art class. And loving it."

Stella felt a little proud of herself, even if she knew it was inappropriate, as Kelsey clearly didn't think that was a good thing.

"Why does that bother you?"

Kelsey turned back toward her homework and radio, threatening to drown her mother out once again. "I knew you wouldn't understand."

"Then help me."

Kelsey averted her eyes from Stella's, taking great care not to look at her. Kelsey had always had a habit of doing that when she was sad.

"It's all they talk about anymore. They're going to your class every Saturday. After they finish, they just want to hang out together and draw or paint. They don't invite me to hang out anymore."

Stella didn't really see how that was her own fault, but nevertheless, she felt guilty. "Oh, honey."

"You already moved me here, away from all my friends in Georgia. I had to make all new ones, and it took forever to find people I had anything in common with at all. Now you're taking them, too."

Ah, so that was it. Kelsey was jealous, afraid that her new friends would choose her mother over her and leave her alone again. She'd already dealt with that loneliness earlier in the year, and it had been so difficult. Kelsey wasn't a party animal or anything, but she was a social creature, and if she didn't have friends to chat with and hang out with, she tended to feel trapped and down on herself.

"That's not my intention, honey," Stella explained. "I can't help that your friends took my class. I need to be able to offer these painting lessons for a stable income. It's too hard to rely on selling paintings alone. I need to make sure that I've got something steady."

"I get that," Kelsey conceded. "I just don't understand why you have to steal all my friends in the process."

"I didn't take your friends. They're students in my class. It's not like I'm hanging out with them on the weekends and hitting up parties with them."

Kelsey glared, dark and venomous. "Oh, yeah? They told me you bought them lunch today. We had plans, but they canceled because they wanted to stay after class and help you clean up."

Stella felt guilty about that. "I didn't know you had plans with them. They insisted on cleaning up."

"I just don't understand why you can't make your own

friends. Every time I feel like I have everything together and know what I'm doing with my life, you mess it up!"

Stella's eyes went wide with hurt. She knew her daughter could see, but she didn't rescind her outburst. Instead, she flopped down on her bed and turned away, hugging her pillow close to her chest.

"Kelsey, that's not fair."

"I told you I didn't want to talk."

Stella nodded. There was no use in pushing because she had a feeling she'd only be hurt worse if she did.

"Okay. I'll... come back later. I ordered pizza for dinner. I'll text you when it gets here."

She left Kelsey's room, closing the door all the way behind her and feeling tears spring to her eyes once she was safely on the other side. This was just teenage angst, she told herself. Kelsey was upset and hurt, and she was taking it out on Stella. That didn't mean that she was a bad mother, or that what Kelsey was saying was true, even if the feelings were.

Was it true, though, she wondered? She hadn't made any attempt to steal Kelsey's friends, but she had to admit it did appear as though Joey and Dani were close. She was sure that the art classes were only bringing them closer together. If they really were bonding over a hobby that Kelsey didn't share, it made sense that she'd feel left out, especially given that their love of art was driving them right into Stella's path.

Maybe this was her fault. Perhaps she should have thought ahead and admitted only Dani or Joey, not both. She'd known at the time that they were Kelsey's friends, she just hadn't thought it would be a problem. When she'd bought them lunch, it was just appreciation for them helping her clean up. But in retrospect, she should have turned them away and told them she didn't want help. That way, they would have kept their plans with Kelsey, and maybe she wouldn't be so upset and hurt now.

"Stella?" Gwen's voice called, and Stella wiped furiously at her teary eyes as she sat on the couch, not wanting Gwen to see that she was upset.

"Yeah, hi, Gwen," she replied, trying for casualness and falling short. "How was the beach?"

Gwen frowned. "You look like you've been crying," she said, and Stella shook her head, exhaling a shaky sigh.

"No, of course not."

Gwen sat down next to her on the couch, softly putting one hand over Stella's knee, anger suddenly forgotten in the wake of crisis. "You can't lie to me, sweetheart. I know you. What happened?"

Stella shook her head. "It's stupid. Just a little argument with Kelsey. Nothing major. You know how teenagers can be."

"Yes," Gwen admitted, "I do. And I know how it can break your heart when they're acting out. What did you two argue about?"

Stella took a steadying breath. "It's nothing really," she began, but Gwen wasn't convinced, and she buckled under the scrutinizing look. "Just... she's upset because she feels like I'm stealing her friends. Two of her friends from college are taking my art class and, apparently, it's brought them close enough that they're not hanging out with her as often."

Gwen looked confused. "Well, that doesn't sound like your fault."

Stella averted her eyes, feeling guilty. "They have been spending a lot of time around the studio," she admitted. "Today, both of them insisted on helping me clean up after class, so I bought them lunch as a thank you for the assistance. I didn't realize they were supposed to have plans with Kelsey, and they canceled."

"That's hard," Gwen said, "but it's still not your fault. How were you supposed to know?"

"I just feel guilty. I should have—"

"There's nothing you could or should have done differently in this situation," she curtailed Stella's self-deprecation. "Being a mom is hard. Kelsey is going through a difficult time with her friends, and it must be difficult to watch her go through that, but that doesn't make it your fault."

"I'm the one who pulled her away from her friends in Atlanta."

"No, you're not," Gwen said. She specifically did not blame Jeff for that, even if it was somewhat his fault, but it was still nice to hear someone say that it wasn't her wrongdoing. "These things happen. Kids move with their parents all the time. I was an army brat; did you know that? My dad served, and we were constantly moving around the country, as he was called to different bases. Every few years, I had to move to a different city and leave behind all my friends and make new ones. I blamed my mother for it at the time because my dad wasn't often around for me to be angry with. Now that I'm grown, I know it wasn't their fault. With a little distance, I recognize that my mother was doing what she had to do and what she thought would be best for me. And you know what? I appreciate her for it. She was right."

Stella smiled. "I didn't know that about you," she said. "And that does help."

"Of course," Gwen added, "as a child, I had wished that my mother would just keep us in one place. It was my father who needed to move, not us, so I always wondered why she was always making all of us move. But I'm glad that she kept the family together. I would have missed my daddy."

There it was, Stella thought, the sinking feeling that even though Gwen didn't blame her, she wasn't fully approving of her choices. Maybe she had a point, Stella thought. She wasn't sure if it was the moment of weakness that was causing her to feel this way or the fact that it appeared as though no one was on her side, but she wondered, not for the first time, if she was really making the right choice. She'd moved with Kelsey to Sunrise Beach to escape the press and the media attention plus the fact that she could no longer afford that big mansion in Atlanta. At the time, it had felt like the only option. The farther away from the scandal she was able to move the two of them, the better Kelsey's life would be for it.

Now, she couldn't help but wonder if that choice was selfish. Even with all things considered, did Kelsey need her father in her life? He was in prison, but Gwen was right —that wouldn't be forever. He was likely going to get out sooner rather than later, as he'd been eligible for parole, and Stella couldn't see any reason that he wouldn't be accepted. After all, he had no prior arrests. Jeff barely even had parking tickets, for crying out loud. Before everything, he'd been a model citizen, and his story about trying to make enough money to be able to pay for college for his gifted daughter might be sympathetic to a parole board.

"Thanks, Gwen," she said finally. "You've given me a lot to think about."

Gwen looked pleased. She reached over and pulled Stella in for a tight, if brief, hug.

"You can always come to me with these things, darling," she said. "Family is family, and there's nothing you could do or say that would make me turn my back on family."

Stella couldn't help but wonder if that was what she was doing to Jeff. Was she really overreacting to his lies, his criminal behavior? If Gwen, the woman who raised him and instilled values of hard work and honesty into him, could forgive him for this, should she find it in her heart to do the same?

# Chapter Twelve

Stella hadn't heard from Maisie since she'd left for California several days ago. She'd expected a text when Maisie's plane landed—she had always liked for friends and family to check in when they arrived home whether they were driving or flying. Maisie had reassured her that she would send a message when she got back home.

Oh, well, Stella thought. Surely, Maisie was busy. She was a successful art saleswoman and had friends and family of her own. More than likely, she was just busy. Still, Stella couldn't help but feel uneasy. She didn't want to bombard Maisie with texts or anything, but she had left with several of Stella's paintings, and Stella had hoped to at least hear confirmation that they hadn't been lost in customs or something at the airport. Taking expensive valuables on an airplane was nerve-wracking, and she hoped that the reason she wasn't hearing from Maisie wasn't because something had happened to her art, and she didn't want to tell Stella about it.

In truth, Stella was hoping to hear back sooner rather

than later because she really wanted a distraction from the thoughts still plaguing her mind. Ever since the last conversation she had had with Gwen, Stella hadn't been able to stop thinking about Jeff and whether or not she'd made the right choice.

Well, that wasn't quite true. She knew that divorcing him had been the right decision. She hadn't wanted to, but given what he'd done to their family, he'd broken her trust, and she couldn't stay married to someone she couldn't trust. No, it wasn't the decision she'd made at the time that worried her. It was the one she was making right now, the ones she was making every day—her decision to keep Jeff out of her life, out of Kelsey's life.

Gwen had made a point about how there was nothing in the world that Jeff could do that would make her stop loving him as her son, and it had made Stella think. Of course, she felt the same way about Kelsey. If her own daughter had been involved in some kind of criminal activity, she would give her the benefit of the doubt. She would have no trouble believing in her heart of hearts that Kelsey had nothing but good intentions, so why was she finding it so difficult to extend that to Jeff?

When they'd gotten married, she'd promised him unconditional love. She'd sworn to love him for better or worse, in richer and poorer. Was she going back on that promise by not talking to him to hear him out?

A big part of her felt as though there was just nothing that Jeff could say that would change the past, and that was an enormous part of her hesitation. She had already heard from his own lips why he had embezzled the money. When he'd made his guilty plea, he'd been allowed to make a statement before the sentencing. He'd sworn that he'd only done it because he was afraid that he couldn't provide the life that Kelsey deserved, that she was going to grow up and want to go to an Ivy League school. He wanted to make sure that she didn't have to wonder whether they could afford it.

Honestly, she'd thought it was sort of a hollow excuse at the time. They'd had lots of conversations about options, anywhere from student loans to dipping into Stella's nest egg from her parents to Stella going back to work and helping to pad the college fund with another income. Kelsey could have worked jobs during the summer, and there were always scholarships for students in their difficult position, even if they were very few, and the ones that did exist were highly competitive. The point wasn't that he had made a bad choice, but that he'd done it without consulting Stella first. He'd known that she wouldn't approve, so rather than use that knowledge to make the right choice, he'd decided instead to be secretive about it. She couldn't trust him again knowing that he was capable of lying to her for years.

Gwen wasn't letting up, though. She was firm on her stance that Stella and Jeff belonged together, and Stella was beginning to think that her visit was a little less innocuous than she'd originally believed. Had trying to get Stella to forgive Jeff been the plan all along? Stella sighed, stirring the eggs she was cooking for breakfast while she could hear everyone shuffling around their bedrooms.

"I think you should call him today," came Gwen's voice suddenly from behind Stella, almost startling her. She blinked in surprise, then turned around to see Gwen standing in her nightgown, her phone in hand with Jeff's number pulled up.

"What? Gwen, come on. I'm not calling Jeff right now."

"After breakfast then," she said firmly. Stella felt a confusing combination of ire and a desire to appease her mother-in-law, with whom she had only just reconciled the night before. "Last night, you were so distraught about how difficult it is raising a teenager on your own. You needed advice, not to mention comfort, and I was more than happy to give that to you. But Stella, I'm not going to be here forever. I'm going back to Atlanta soon. When I do, who are you going to turn to for things like that?"

Stella's mouth hung open in shock. Was Gwen really using the ill-timed breakdown she'd had about her argument with Kelsey as a tool for getting her to think she should call Jeff?

"What kind of advice is Jeff going to be able to offer from jail?" she demanded. "How is he going to comfort me from a prison cell? It's not like he's going to be here to throw his arms around me and tell me it will all be okay."

"Maybe not immediately," Gwen conceded, "but he won't be in jail forever. I've been writing to the parole board. He's eligible for it soon, and a letter from you would certainly strengthen his case." She sighed, sitting down at the table and taking a sip from the mug of coffee that Stella had laid out for her. "I raised a child on my own," she said, "and it was difficult. I wasn't there often enough. I worry that's why he did what he did."

Stella's heart broke. "Gwen, we've talked about this. That's not your fault, just like it's not mine or Kelsey's. Jeff made his bed, and now he's lying in it."

Gwen nodded. "That may be so," she admitted, "but ultimately, it's not as if he hurt anyone. This is forgivable, Stella. And I think it's time."

Stella felt anger, hot and red and dizzying, flash through her. She could smell that the eggs were burning, but she didn't care.

"You think he didn't hurt anyone?" she argued. "He hurt me. He hurt you and Kelsey. He hurt a lot of people. It's not a victimless crime."

"I'm just making the point that it's not as if he's some sort of violent criminal."

Stella sighed, pinching the bridge of her nose in frustration. That wasn't the problem, she thought. She wasn't afraid of Jeff, and she never had been. It was that he broke her trust, and she wasn't sure they could come back from that. No matter how many ways she explained that to Gwen, she simply wasn't understanding it, and it was beginning to get unacceptable.

"I divorced Jeff for a reason," Stella finally said. "You might not agree with that, and that's fine, but I didn't make my choice lightly. I knew we were married for over twenty years, and separating from him was the hardest thing I've ever had to do. It broke my heart in more ways than one, and of course, I wonder all the time what might have happened if I'd made a different choice. Should I have caught on sooner? Was it something I said that made him think he had to do that for us?" When Gwen didn't respond, she continued. "The one thing I am sure about is that I made the right choice by getting a divorce. It was hard enough to lose everything we owned without having to think about having a husband in prison. I had to stop worrying about him to survive, and I'm not willing to reopen the relationship. Period."

Gwen looked more hurt than angry, but she didn't say a word. Instead, she stood from the table, not bothering to wait around for the breakfast which was now equal parts burnt and cold from having taken the time to argue. Stella felt guilty, but at the same time, this wasn't Gwen's business to push. If she didn't feel like she could be around their home without picking this same fight over and over, then maybe it was just time for her to go home. If she was only being kind to Stella because she thought there was a chance she could convince her to get back with Jeff, maybe it was time for Stella to cut her losses and come to terms with the fact that she'd not just lost her husband through all this, but the woman in her life that had been more of a mother to her than anyone else.

Stella didn't feel much like going to the gallery, so instead, she decided to do some cleaning around the house. Gwen had been lending a hand with it while she was staying, but sometimes, Stella just needed to get her hands dirty and deep-clean her living space in order to feel better about herself. She donned a pair of rubber gloves and sprayed nearly the whole kitchen down with Lysol until she was a bit dizzy from the fumes, then went to work scrubbing.

Gwen didn't come out of her room for the rest of the day, and Kelsey had gone out with friends. She'd been doing that more and more lately. So much so, in fact, that she was rarely home anymore. Stella assumed that it was just a normal side effect of being a teenager, and she hadn't had too much of a problem with it until Kelsey had started missing her curfew.

Stella liked to believe that she had set up a very reasonable curfew. She was a bit of a night owl herself, so allowing Kelsey to stay out until 11:30 was fairly easy for her to swing, every once in a while, without feeling like she was forcing herself to stay awake just to make sure Kelsey came home safely. She had always been good about her curfew before, when she was still living with Jeff. Stella supposed it helped that most of her friends at the time had earlier curfews than Kelsey's own, so she was usually home about an hour before she needed to be anyway. She'd only been late a handful of times, and even then, it had always been only by a few minutes, nothing Stella had ever felt the need to punish. Traffic happened, sometimes, and she wasn't strict on her for things that were beyond her control.

Now, however, Kelsey was staying out much later than she was meant to. On a good night, she'd be home by 11:45, and on a bad one, sometimes it could be 1:00 in the morning before she walked through the door. At first, Stella had suspected that she might be out drinking, but she never looked intoxicated or smelled like alcohol. When she asked what she'd been doing, Kelsey always told her that she was studying with friends or watching movies at someone's house.

Tonight, Stella was sitting up in the living room, feeling antsy and nervous and alone. It was past 1:00, and she hadn't so much as heard from Kelsey. She'd tried calling her phone and sending her texts, which she read but did not reply to. It was beginning to make Stella feel fearful.

Just when she was contemplating waking Gwen to see

if they should call the police and report her as a missing person, simply because this was just so unlike Kelsey, she heard the keys jingle in the door. She let out a breath that she hadn't even felt that she was holding.

"Kelsey Britton," she hissed sternly, causing Kelsey to jump, startled. "Where were you?"

"Out," she replied curtly. Her hair was done neatly, and she was wearing makeup which made Stella anxious for the first time that perhaps she might have been seeing a boy. She felt stupid that the thought hadn't crossed her mind sooner, but this was *Kelsey*. Her daughter, so brilliant, so bright. She would never do anything that would put herself in any danger, right?

Sometimes, Kelsey was so smart that Stella could forget a bit that she was still barely more than a child. Other times, however, that glaring immaturity and lack of knowledge about the way the world works was obvious. This was one of those times.

"Out," Stella echoed. Kelsey nodded, a terse, irritable motion.

"Yeah, out. You said I could go."

"I said you could go if you were back by 11:30," Stella reminded her. "Do you have any idea what time it is?"

Kelsey shrugged like she didn't know or didn't care. "You didn't have to wait up for me. I'm not a baby."

"Oh, I know you're not," Stella agreed angrily. "Which is exactly why I expect you to know better than this. You really expect me to go to bed not having any idea where you are? Without even hearing from you?"

"You went five years with no idea what Dad was

doing," Kelsey snapped, "so why should you start paying attention now?"

Stella's mouth dropped open. She was glad Gwen was asleep, as it was the only thing preventing her from going off the handle completely and shouting at her daughter which she knew she'd regret later.

"I need to know who you're going out with this late every night. Are you seeing someone? A boy?"

Kelsey rolled her eyes. "It's a group of people from school, Mom. There are boys there, yeah."

Stella felt a knot in her stomach unclench slightly, feeling satisfied to know that at least Kelsey wasn't alone with some guy so late at night in a dangerous situation.

"Do I know these friends?"

Kelsey laughed once, bitter and humorless. "Probably, since it seems like you're buddies with all the other teenagers in the city!" she whisper-shouted. Under a scrutinizing, serious glare, she deflated. "No. You took all my other friends, so I had to make new ones. Forgive me if I don't want to introduce them to you, so you can steal these away from me, too."

"You know what? You're grounded," Stella said. It had been a long time, perhaps even years, since she'd last grounded Kelsey. She so rarely did anything to deserve punishment. When she got the occasional bad grade in high school, she was always so beaten up about it that Stella never had to punish her. Usually, she had to convince Kelsey not to be so hard on herself more often than she had to punish her.

"Grounded?" Kelsey repeated. "Seriously? Did you forget I'm not in high school any more?"

"Yes, I do remember. I don't care how old you are, I'm not allowing you to behave like this or talk to me this way. You're allowed to go to school and back, nothing else. No hanging out with friends for a week."

"Not like I have any anyway! I can't believe you!" she said as she stomped off in a huff toward her room. Stella sighed, feeling exhausted from more than just the late night.

Great, she thought. As if she didn't have enough to worry about. She only hoped that Gwen wouldn't try to use this against her as leverage to convince her to get back together with Jeff. Feeling as much like a failure as she was feeling now, she might even consider it. Maybe she really *did* need help.

# Chapter Thirteen

Stella tried to reach out to Maisie several times throughout the week, and none of her attempts were successful. She emailed, texted, and called, all to no avail. By Wednesday, she'd decided that her art was officially missing. Now that it was Saturday once more, marking a full week of radio silence, she was pretty sure that the reality was worse than that.

More than anything, she felt stupid. She'd given her art to Maisie with no down-payment, lured in by her promise of having to do no footwork to profit off her art. Something she'd thought so many times in the wake of everything that had happened with Jeff ran through her head over and over: if it sounds too good to be true, it probably is. Jeff's incredible promotion that decided to pay him double and eventually more than triple his starting salary for the same amount of work had been like a dream to her at the time. It had come right at a time when they were so worried about money, and she hadn't questioned it even though hindsight told her she should have. Everyone had reassured her that

Jeff betraying her trust was not her fault and that believing her husband did not make her gullible, and she'd only just begun to internalize it when everything happened.

Stella was beginning to question if she truly was the most gullible person in the world. Maisie had given her this incredible business opportunity, and she hadn't even bothered to Google her name. Maisie had sent her the link to her online gallery, and Stella had decided that was enough. Now, she was kicking herself for not bothering to dig deeper.

With Kelsey and Gwen both giving her the silent treatment, Stella decided that she needed some support from Felicia. She'd apologized for bothering her when she was probably trying to prepare for her brother to come into town, but Felicia had reassured her that she didn't mind. She was startled by how upset Stella had sounded on the phone and invited her over to her own home, promising they'd get to the bottom of it. They were sipping wine at Felicia's breakfast bar in her kitchen, both crowded around her laptop.

"So, she's sent you this website," Felicia said, "and that's all you've got on her, right?"

Stella nodded, placing her head in her hands. "I feel like an idiot."

"No," Felicia said sternly. "This isn't your fault, Stella. I mean it. Not to brag or anything, but I'm a bit of an internet sleuth. We're going to get to the bottom of this."

"I tried Googling Maisie Washington, but I got so many results."

"Well, what else do you have on her? We'll try 'Maisie Washington, art,'" she said, and Stella perked up.

"I know she's from West Covina, California. Does that help?"

"Immensely!" Felicia exclaimed. Stella watched as Felicia Googled the name with all the other information several times, placing quotations around different things and adding and subtracting keywords to try to narrow it down. In the end, the only thing that came up that was verifiably connected to the Maisie that Stella had met was the website displaying all her art.

"Looks as though she's used a fake name," Felicia sighed. "That makes this harder since we've no idea who she really is. Any ideas?"

Stella nodded, clicking back to the tab that contained the website she'd been sent. "Kelsey taught me this," she said. "There are these websites where you can upload an image and reverse-search it."

Felicia frowned. "What does that mean?"

"You can figure out if it's been uploaded somewhere else before. That way, if she has another site with her art where she uses her real name, we can find it."

She uploaded the first photograph of a painting from Maisie's website. Felicia and Stella were silent as they waited for the reverse image search to return anything on the image, and when they did, Stella squealed in excitement.

"There's a hit!" she exclaimed. When she clicked the link, her excitement turned to disappointment as she realized that this website certainly did not belong to Maisie, but a different artist entirely. This one appeared to be some old man who lived in Colorado.

"Let's try another," Felicia encouraged, and Stella,

though she couldn't help but feel like she'd been duped twice, complied. This one returned a portfolio for a college student in South Africa. The third was a painting done by a young woman living in Mexico, and the fourth, a young man who taught himself to paint with his mouth after losing both hands in an accident. Stella felt like crying.

"I can't believe I didn't even notice they weren't the same artist," she said. "What kind of artist wouldn't notice that these were all painted by different people? It's so obvious now."

Felicia rubbed Stella's back in comforting circles. "Someone who wasn't looking to catch someone in a lie," she replied. "What reason would you have had to give her the third degree like this? It would have been rude."

"Rude or not, I wouldn't be down five of my favorite paintings," she pointed out. "Is there something wrong with me? Something that lets people know they can get away with telling me a lie?"

Felicia shook her head, pulling Stella in for a closer hug. "Oh, darling, of course not," she reassured. "It's bad luck. But you're not to blame for it."

Stella didn't feel much like hanging out and drinking wine anymore. Though she'd felt that she needed the support to investigate, she really just wanted to be left alone once she'd gotten to the bottom of everything. This was her fault, and now she had to go back home to a house full of people who were angry at her for other things she'd managed to bungle.

She felt as though it was impossible for her to catch a break these days. No matter what she did, someone was always getting hurt. Gwen was hurt by her decision not to go back to Jeff. She'd hurt Kelsey by inadvertently taking her friends away from her with her art class.

"I think I might head home." She excused herself, and Felicia knew her well enough not to argue.

"Okay, Stella. You'll call if you need anything, all right?"

Stella nodded, but she was sure that she probably wouldn't call, too embarrassed at the sheer number of things she felt like she was mishandling right now.

She didn't head home. Instead, she went to the beach. In the dark, Sunrise Beach looked much different than it did during the day. The bustling crowds were gone, and it felt more natural, quieter. She sat in the sand, grabbing handfuls of it and feeling as the grains slipped through her fingers. More and more things seemed to be doing that lately.

During the day, this part of town was always loud and crowded, but right now, there were hardly any people around. She was sure that if she walked along the shore to a larger part of town, there would be more night owls doing activities this late, but the part of town she lived in was fairly tame. Most people owned shops around here, so they were all in bed sleeping, waiting to open early the next morning. Stella should be doing the same, but she knew that she wouldn't be able to sleep even if she did go home now. Her head was a mess.

As she watched the moon sit atop the waves, reflected in the water below it, she thought about all the fears she'd had when she moved here. She'd been afraid that Kelsey would never forgive her for uprooting her life, that she would never be able to find success in her art, that she would always feel like she was running from her own reputation and, more importantly, from Jeff's. All those fears had been realized, but after addressing them, they had each fallen away from her consciousness. Just a few months ago, her relationship with Kelsey had been better than it had been in years. She'd taken a risk and opened the gallery which had resulted in the exhibit that had attracted people from near and far. She'd even come to terms with the possibility of her reputation following her around. In order to go through with the exhibit and advertise it by tossing her name out to the public, she'd needed to overcome that fear, and after she had, she'd felt free. Stella had really felt happier than she had since the divorce, but now, that heavy feeling was back to crush her.

What good was it to make up with Kelsey if she was only going to ruin it again? Could she really consider her art career a success when she was out here giving her art away for free to a person who had planned from the beginning to run off with it and never speak to her again?

# Chapter Fourteen

When Gwen announced that she was going back home, Stella couldn't help but feel a little relieved. Things had been so tense for the past week, and every moment she spent in her house had been uncomfortable. She'd been escaping to the gallery as often as possible, but of course, she couldn't hide out there all day. She had a child to feed.

A child who wasn't speaking to her, either. Most nights, Stella would arrive home to make dinner, sometimes finding that Gwen had already taken care of that without even notifying Stella and call for Kelsey to come out of her room. She would, but when Stella tried to say anything to her, she just took her food and mumbled some lie about having homework to do. Stella knew that wasn't true, but what could she say?

Gwen would eat with her, but she often wanted to bring up Jeff again. When Stella made it clear that she didn't want to discuss that topic again, Gwen would get huffy and not want to talk about anything at all. That usually left Stella sitting at the kitchen island by herself, picking at a cold dinner and resigning to go to bed early to read until she fell asleep. She certainly didn't feel like painting. Moods like this sapped her creativity, as the more she tried to connect with her emotions to transfer them to canvas, the more she wanted to curl up in a ball and not move ever again.

That night, as she lay in bed trying to concentrate on her book, the sound of someone creeping down the hallway filled her with hope for a moment. Maybe Kelsey finally wanted to talk. This was how they often made up, after all —Kelsey would eventually feel guilty for being so hard on her mother and curl up in bed beside her. Stella would turn on her TV and they'd watch some low-budget, feel-good movie together.

"Come on in," she said, hoping to see her daughter standing in the precipice and feeling dejected when her mother-in-law appeared in front of her on the couch.

Right. Kelsey wasn't even home. Stella had completely forgotten that she'd allowed Kelsey to stay over at her friend's house since it was Saturday night, and she didn't have school the next morning. "Oh, Gwen. Is everything okay?"

Gwen nodded. She was wearing her floor-length, pink silk nightgown, which had belonged to her mother. Stella had a lot of memories of crying into that gown right after her own parents had passed.

"I just wanted to let you know I bought my plane ticket," she announced, and Stella nodded.

"Right," she replied. What was there to say? "When is your flight?"

"The morning after tomorrow." Wow, Stella thought,

that was soon. "I fear I might have overstayed my welcome."

Stella wanted to tell her that she hadn't overstayed, just overstepped a few boundaries, but that would only upset her further.

"You know you're always welcome here."

Gwen nodded as if she'd barely heard her. "Well, my flight is at 8:00 in the morning, so if you wouldn't mind, I could use a driver."

"Of course. I'll take you. Just let me know if you need help packing or anything."

"I will." Gwen sat beside her on the sofa which made Stella think for a moment that Gwen might apologize. She was big on the idea of never going to bed angry and that family was the most important thing in the world. If Stella was lucky, Gwen would forgive her before she let herself go back home. "You know I love you, don't you?" she asked. "More than just my son's wife. You've been like a daughter to me."

Stella nodded, feeling hot tears well up behind her eyes and hoping that it was too dark in the living room for Gwen to see them. "I love you like a mother, too, Gwen."

"Then you'll understand why I've been so pushy on this. I love my son more than anything, and you're the best thing that ever happened to him. You made him a father, and I know he's never stopped loving you. The fact that you've iced him out over all of this has been tearing him apart, and it kills me to see him so broken up. I'm truly trying to do what's best for the both of you. If I didn't believe that he was sorry, I wouldn't be trying to get you two back together."

Stella nodded. "It's not about whether he's sorry. I know he is. I knew he was the moment he was arrested. It's the fact that he wasn't sorry until he got in trouble that I can't get past."

To Stella's surprise, for the first time, Gwen's eyes fill with tears. "I raised my boy right," she said, "and I just hate to see him lose everything over a mistake."

Stella didn't know what to say, but luckily, or maybe unluckily, she didn't have to. Gwen said that she was going to get some sleep and left the room, retreating back to Stella's bedroom. Stella wanted to follow, but that was never a good idea with Gwen. If she could, she'd tell her that she didn't think for one moment that what Jeff did was Gwen's fault. She did believe he knew right from wrong, but he thought he could get away with embezzlement and that it would be a victimless crime. He'd managed to tell himself that they really needed the money and that embezzling was the right thing to do. Once he was in jail, he probably had changed his tune, but it would be impossible for Stella to ever be with him again. She couldn't live a life where she was always looking over her shoulder, always feeling as though she had to double-check whatever her husband was up to just to make sure it wasn't shady. She deserved better than that, and he deserved to make a fresh start when he was released, too, with someone who could see past his criminal past. That just wasn't Stella.

They'd both be happy again, she hoped. Stella had thought she had achieved that, but as it turned out, the joy she'd found was only temporary. She was in yet another hole that she didn't know how to dig herself out of.

. . .

The next day, Kelsey didn't come home in the morning like she'd said she would. Instead, she sent a text saying that she was going to stay out until dinner which Stella replied was fine. Now wasn't the time to be pushing Kelsey to hang around the house, especially with Gwen so sad. It was probably best that everyone had a little distance from one another.

Stella worked around the house and the gallery all day, but when dinner rolled around, instead of Kelsey walking through the door, her phone vibrated with yet another text.

**staying at mariah's another night**

Stella blinked. It was a Sunday, she thought. Kelsey hadn't even brought the car, as Mariah had picked her up.

**Call me.**

She got a notification that Kelsey had read the message, but Stella's phone didn't ring. She tried calling Kelsey, and when her first call was not answered, her irritation turned to panic.

"Kelsey, this isn't like you, and I need to hear your voice telling me that you're okay. Please call me back." She hesitated. "I love you," she finished before hanging up the phone. Anxiously, she waited for the phone to ring, which it did, not ten minutes later.

"Kelsey," she breathed a sigh of relief. "Is everything okay?"

"Yeah," she snapped. "I'm fine. I'm just staying at Mariah's house again tonight."

Stella shook her head even though Kelsey couldn't see it. "No, you're not," she replied. "It's a school night."

"We go to the same school," Kelsey reminded her as if

that were the only problem. Her tone was snippy and disrespectful. "I'm going to carpool with her."

"You're going to come home tonight," Stella demanded firmly. "Grandma is leaving tomorrow morning, and you're going to be here to say good-bye."

"I'll call her."

"Come home."

"No. I'm an adult! You can't make me do something I don't want to do."

"I can as long as you're living under my roof."

Kelsey huffed a sarcastic, humorless laugh. "What are you going to do? Come force me to go home?"

Kelsey hung up without another word, and Stella reached for her keys, wanting nothing more than to rush over to Mariah's house and do just that—force Kelsey to come back home. Her father had once done that to her when she was a teenager. Stella had been sixteen at the time and promised that she would return home from the park before dark. She'd just received her driver's license and was enjoying the new freedom it provided, specifically in being allowed to see boys after school. That was something her parents had always been strict about, but of course, it didn't stop her from wanting it. She'd only just met Jeff, and she already had a huge crush on him.

Jeff was a little older than her and, because he was a boy, allowed a lot more freedom than she was. Jeff could go for walks after dark with his friends. He could hang out at the park as late as he wanted, so long as he was home before Gwen fell asleep. To Stella's sixteen-year-old mind, it felt as though she had the strictest, most unfair parents in the entire world.

Not half an hour after dark that night, while Stella and her friends were still sitting around in the park gazebo, laughing and telling stupid stories under the streetlight, she'd become distantly aware that there was a man in the park who seemed to be on a mission. She could only barely see him, stopping everyone he passed and showing them a photograph from his pocket. Most of them shook their heads afterward. For a moment, she assumed that he was looking for a missing toddler or something, and her heart bled for him.

That only lasted a moment until the next person that the man talked to pointed toward the gazebo. He'd begun walking toward them, and she'd gone stock still in mortification as realization set in.

"Hey, Stella, isn't that your old man?" one of her friends had asked when he'd gotten close enough for them all to see his face. Stella's own face had been beet red.

Her father had stopped a few feet away from the gazebo and pointed to his watch, not even bothering to come all the way up and verbally demand that she leave.

"I think I've got to go," she'd said hastily, feeling more humiliated than she ever had in her life. That night, her father had given her a lecture about curfew. Thinking back on it now, as a parent, she understood. It had been the first time that Stella had done such a thing, and he'd genuinely thought that she might be a missing person. There were a lot of crazy people out there, he'd said. She had to be careful.

Stella had never made that mistake again, but it hadn't come without a price. Her relationship with her father had forever changed, and she'd never felt safe to tell him much after that. It had planted the seed of doubt that if he didn't approve of her choices, he would make it a public matter. When he had passed away just two years later, Stella felt a lot of guilt for having let the incident cause such a rift between them.

Reluctantly, she set her keys back in her purse. As much as she knew Kelsey needed to be disciplined right now, this wasn't the way to do it. The only thing she would accomplish by driving down to Mariah's house and demanding her daughter come home was pushing her further away. Regardless of how much she hated Kelsey's behavior, Stella didn't want to make her feel as though she couldn't talk to her. For now, she would just have to wait for Kelsey to come back home and deal with her then.

The next day, Stella woke up early to go running. She'd been slacking on that front a bit, opting instead to cook breakfast for Gwen, but today, she decided that she would forgo cooking. Gwen probably wouldn't want to eat with her, anyway.

As she jogged along the beach, Stella passed some of the people she'd gotten to know in her time here in Sunrise Beach. She waved to Mr. and Mrs. Jeong as they got everything ready to open their convenience store for the day, and to Jessica, her friend whose father rented her the space for her gallery.

"Good morning," Stella called, her voice more chipper than she felt. Everyone around here was always so happy. It was refreshing, for sure, but sometimes she felt as though she was the only person in the whole town whose life wasn't perfect all the time. Logically, she knew that couldn't be true, but a lot of the time, that was the way it felt. How did all this come so naturally to other people, so easily? Did all the other mothers wonder if they were doing everything wrong? Did the other artists have so many doubts?

Stella stopped home for a quick shower and to grab a breakfast of untoasted PopTarts, which she ate on her walk to the gallery. Eating processed junk like that might as well negate her running, but today, she didn't care. The taste was comforting. She associated them mostly with her childhood when things were simpler.

By the time she had arrived at her gallery, she had finished breakfast and even stopped for a latte in the cafe that Jessica ran with her sister. Stella was cleaning and sipping her coffee, getting ready for her class that was to begin in just over an hour, when the doorbell rang with someone entering the shop. She thought that was odd because as she was preparing for class, she hadn't yet switched the sign to "open." She turned around, expecting to have to tell a perspective customer that they would have to come back later, and instead found herself face to face with two of her students: Joey and Dani, Kelsey's friends.

"Hey, guys," she greeted. "It's a little early for class, you know." She hoped they weren't stopping in to help her set up. Given how angry Kelsey had been when she'd let them stay late to clean, Stella couldn't imagine how she'd feel if she let it happen again.

"Yeah, we know, sorry," Dani said. She seemed apprehensive, a tone that Stella had never seen the normally boisterous young girl use. Dani was one of the bubbliest people that Stella had ever met, so to see her standing there, looking down at her feet nervously and wringing her hands, Stella knew that was something very wrong.

"What's going on?" she asked, moving forward and pushing her new rolling office chair toward Dani to take a seat. "Are you all right?"

Dani nodded, then looked to Joey. He was a bit quieter, in general, but the somber mood was unusual for him, as well. Stella felt her heart rate beginning to pick up, and it wasn't just the caffeine.

"We're fine," Joey reassured, which didn't do much in the way of calming Stella's nerves. "It's just that we've got some bad news." Stella's mind began to run with worst-case scenarios. She'd come to care for these kids as if they were her own, and that meant worrying about them like they were hers, too.

"What happened?"

"We're dropping the class!" Dani suddenly blurted out. Stella blinked in surprise, torn between feeling confused and grateful that no one was hurt.

"Okay," she said. "Can I ask why? If it's a financial thing, we can work something out."

"It's not about the money," Joey replied. "It's Kelsey."

"What about Kelsey?"

"We know she's upset that we're taking your class," Dani explained. "She's swearing that she's fine with it, but we all know she's not. You guys have been fighting like crazy ever since we enrolled, right?"

"That's not something you two need to be concerned about. It's not your fault."

"I mean, maybe it's not our fault, but we can fix it," Joey

said. "If we weren't in your class anymore, you guys wouldn't be fighting, right?"

Stella wanted to tell them that wasn't true. Her relationship with Kelsey had been improving before the art classes, sure, but the solution to her anger wasn't for her friends to drop out. Sometimes, with raising children, appeasing them and giving them what they want just to stop a tantrum wasn't the best option. It wasn't as though Kelsey was throwing a tantrum—her feelings were understandable and legitimate. However, she needed to learn that her friends were allowed to have hobbies without her. Just because something hurt her feelings, that didn't mean that it was someone else's obligation to fix it.

Stella couldn't say all that, though. It would humiliate Kelsey, as well as make her seem like she was begging her students to stay in a class they had clearly made up their minds to leave. She didn't want to seem pathetic.

"If that's really what you want," she said, and Dani shook her head. She looked close to tears, but whether that was from the decision or the discomfort of confrontation was anyone's guess.

"Of course it's not what we want," she said. "We love your class. It's just that we love Kelsey more, and we don't want to make it worse if this is hurting her."

Stella sighed. If there was a silver lining to this, she supposed it was the fact that she was glad Kelsey had found such good friends, ones that would make a selfless decision on her behalf without asking for praise in return.

"Well, I certainly appreciate you caring so much about my daughter's feelings."

"It's not just for her!" Dani quickly added. "For you,

too. Kelsey used to talk about you all the time, before she was so mad. You gave up a lot for her, and we know you love her a lot. We just want you both to be able to bury the hatchet."

"If you ever change your minds, my door is always open." Stella had only barely started thinking about the possibility of offering more classes, and of course, with two of her students unlikely to re-enroll, that made it a little more difficult to justify the decision. There was an enormous possibility that she wouldn't make enough to break even on the cost of supplies if one or two more people decided not to move forward with another class.

With another onslaught of apologies, Dani and Joey shuffled out the door, leaving Stella alone and in no mood to teach in an hour. She'd already been digging deep just to find the energy to conduct class, but after speaking with Dani and Joey, she felt even worse. Things just kept getting harder. Was that ever going to stop? When would she finally catch a break?

She downed the rest of her latte as she debated whether to cancel class for the day, making up some excuse of a stomach bug or needing to help Gwen pack for the airport. She decided against it, however, when the reality of income slapped her in the face. What was she supposed to do without the steady income of two of her students? What would she do when class ended, and she couldn't risk starting a new one? She simply couldn't afford to take a day off, no matter how much she needed it.

# Chapter Fifteen

Class went well enough. Stella was sure that her remaining three students knew something was bothering her, but everyone elected against mentioning it. One asked where Dani and Joey were, but Stella simply said that they were dropping the class due to school commitments. Everyone seemed to believe that, or if they didn't, they did not ask further questions. She had to admit that things were a lot less fun without them. Dani and Joey, since they were friends outside of class, always brought a positive energy to the group. They were full of jokes, constantly playing around with one another. Dani was so sweet, complimenting the works of everyone else in the class, and Joey was helpful, always willing to offer a hand when someone was struggling to grasp a new concept. Stella missed them.

"Stella, dear," the older woman she taught, Mary, spoke up, pulling her from her thoughts. Mary tended to ask for approval or pointers more often than her other students, so Stella went around to look at the canvas. She quickly found that wasn't what Mary was looking at. She was staring out the glass front door.

"How can I help, Mary?"

"I was going to ask if it would be all right if I skedaddled a little early," she said. "It's looking like it might storm, and you know I live by the bay. I want to make sure I have time to get into my neighborhood before the roads flood."

"Was it supposed to rain today?" another student, a young woman named Imani, asked. "I didn't hear anything about it on the news."

Stella looked outside and saw that the sky was, indeed, rather dark. Stella could see the waves of the ocean, eerily calm in the way they always were before a big storm. The weather hadn't predicted this, but she supposed that was what she got for living next to the ocean. Sometimes, things came up that were unpredictable and unfortunate, and there was nothing that could be done but adapt to the new situation at hand.

"I think we can dismiss class early for the day," she said. "I want everyone to get home safely. If you want, we can stay a little longer next week, so you all can have the time you paid for."

Everyone seemed to agree with that plan and gathered their things without wasting any time. Within five minutes, she was alone in the gallery again. She lived close enough that she didn't mind staying after to make sure everything was put away. Ever since someone had thrown a rock through her window several months ago, even though she was fairly sure that had been a scare tactic to convince her to sell the shop, she'd been wary of leaving any valuables in plain view of the window. It was unfortunate enough that her paintings were on display from the street. She didn't need to add more fuel to the fire.

As she put away the paints and easels, she couldn't help but feel a little glad that the storm had such good timing. She really wasn't feeling up to teaching, and though she'd tried her best, she knew that it had shown. Cutting class short by about half was a bit of a relief.

Before she was able to finish putting everything in its place, the rain began to come down hard. She'd thought she would have more time, but the storm was fast and aggressive. Suddenly, she remembered that she'd walked there instead of driving and regretted not having gone home when she had the chance. She had to decide between waiting out the storm or asking Gwen to bring the car to pick her up, which she wasn't keen on doing. They were already going to have to spend the following morning trapped together on their way to the airport, so why add more tension by starting now?

Stella decided that it would be best to just hunker down and wait out the storm rather than trying to go home. Besides, Gwen, living in Atlanta, would doubtlessly not be used to tropical storms. It had taken Stella a long time to get used to them. Bad storms like this had all felt like hurricanes to her for the first three months, filling her with anxiety. There was no way she would have wanted to drive in a storm like this. It was mild, all things considered, compared to what she knew the coast was capable of, but the rain still fell in huge, unforgiving sheets, and the wind whipped around the trees so hard that they bent slightly. Stella hoped that Gwen and Kelsey were both safe. She figured Gwen wouldn't have gone out by herself, and if she had, she would have made her way back inside at the first sight of a rain cloud. There was nothing she hated more than to get her perm wet. On the other hand, Stella wasn't so sure about Kelsey. She decided to shoot a quick text despite having already settled in her mind that she would leave Kelsey alone.

**Looks like a storm is rolling in. Could be a big one. Does Mariah have supplies if you need to shelter for a bit?**

As angry as Kelsey might have been with her mother, Stella knew that she would reply to a text like this one, and she wasn't disappointed. Less than a minute later, she received a photo of a hurricane supply kit complete with first aid supplies, water, flashlights, food, and gasoline for a generator. She smiled. Kelsey might be young, but she was certainly responsible when it mattered.

**Thank you. Stay safe. Call if you need anything, and text me when the storm hits.**

Kelsey sent back an emoji of a thumbs up without a word, and Stella figured that was as good as she was going to get. She shoved her phone back in her pocket and sighed, sitting in her office chair to watch the storm.

Her gallery had no windows, only a glass door. She was grateful for that, especially after the incident in which a rock had been thrown through the door, as it meant that there were fewer chances for people damaging her studio from the outside or attempting to break in to steal supplies or paintings. Most shops along the beach had small or no windows. When the storms got bad, the wind was likely to send anything from a small stone to an entire trash can through a window, depending on the severity, and no one wanted to deal with that. She had to get closer to the door than she preferred in order to watch the storm, but something about it was enchanting.

She'd painted a storm almost a year ago, when she'd just started the gallery and hadn't even sold her first painting yet. It had been a troubled time for Stella. She and Kelsey weren't getting along, and she'd been wondering if she'd made a mistake leaving Jeff or in trying to make a living as an artist.

She chuckled bitterly to herself. Some things don't change, she thought. After believing she'd conquered all those problems, she was facing them once again. Kelsey had first blamed the move for losing her friends, and now, it was the painting classes. Those very same painting classes, or lack thereof, if she were thinking about the future, were the reason she was once again wondering whether it was crazy to believe she could make a living as an artist. On top of that, her mother-in-law, the person who had been more like a mom than anyone else after her parents had passed, was barely speaking to her.

Stella suddenly felt the urge to paint. Sometimes, she painted because she wanted to remember a feeling or capture a moment. But others because it felt as though her emotions were cooking inside of her, and that if she didn't let out some of the steam, it might boil over. She wasn't sure what would happen if they did. Would she cry? Would she scream? Would she go running back to Jeff, the one person in her life who had ever made her feel safe and protected?

That wasn't something she could think about. It was in the past. Romanticizing it would do her no good. The only thing she could think to do was tear the plastic off a brand-new canvas and set it upon an easel, ready for her to paint the scene outside.

# Chapter Sixteen

Stella had never painted a storm like the one before her. She never really liked to paint the weather. It was an interesting subject, for certain, but it was too difficult to ever really capture. Typically, by the time she was able to get her supplies out and ready, the sky would have already changed, the clouds she had been watching would have moved and shifted, and everything would be back to normal, if a bit dirty from debris and storm damage. This time, Stella was ready. Everything was still set up from class, so she wasted no time, sitting in front of the door with her paints in hand and ready to stare at the sky.

There were layers to a storm, Stella thought. Everything came together into one natural disaster, but just like her life, there were always other factors. There was the wind, which blew down anything in its path, strengthened by the sea. There was the rain, salty and heavy, which came down so hard and so fast that it flooded the streets, overwhelming the rain gutters that were not designed to filter such a downpour. Stella could relate to that, she thought as she fixated on it, painting the enormous puddle forming around the gutter, the lowest point in the street. It was already so full that it wasn't able to keep up, yet it was still being inundated with more rain. She painted each droplet hitting the puddle. Each one might look small, but they added up. Before she knew it, there was so much rain that she felt as though she was begging the storm to slow down, take a break, and give her a chance to catch up.

The thing that no one saw, however, was the structural damage done by storms before this one that weakened the capacity of the city to withstand new hurricanes. Even her studio was damaged. The window that she had replaced was not as strong as the one that had been broken, as the glass had been expensive, and it had happened at a time when money had been a concern. The wood around the foundation had spots of rot from sitting in the water. Some-day, she thought, perhaps the whole building would sink into the ground, needing thousands of dollars of repairs, but not any time soon.

She reminded herself that her own foundation was still healing. Unlike that of the wooden beams that held up the gallery building, she could heal what kept her standing. She had, admittedly, been neglecting that process. Every-thing else had felt more important. Kelsey had been her first priority, then the money, which had also been mostly for Kelsey. She'd been standing on a rotten foundation for a while, just attempting to hold everything together for long enough to weather the storm.

As she painted the rain clouds, she realized that the storm was never going to be over, not really. This one would pass, then another would hit, and she'd be forced to withstand that, too. There was no one she could rely on but herself. Gwen was leaving, and even if she weren't, Stella was too upset to want to reach out for assistance again. Kelsey was barely more than a child, still, and relied upon the support of her mother to see her through things like this. Her friend, Adelle, was gone. Felicia was kind, but in the end, she had her own life and her own problems. Stella needed to find a way to patch up the things that were meant to keep her strong in order to ensure that she could keep standing for years to come.

The storm raged on outside, and Stella found herself less focused on the rain falling from the sky, and more on how it affected the landscape before her. Trees, bent at the base, were not breaking. They were too elastic for that. It would take a true disaster to bowl those over. The rain gutters were full, and some were clogged with leaves, but they were still flowing. Still, as much as the scene outside looked like an enormous mess at the moment, she knew that by tomorrow, everything would look almost normal. In due time, everything would resolve itself. The sky would clear, and the grey clouds would part, leaving behind the sunshine and maybe a rainbow, if she were lucky. The flooding in the streets would diminish until they were all dry once more. The trees would unbend, and her studio would stop shaking in the wind and with every rumble of thunder. Just like she was confident she could wait out the storm, Stella decided that she would weather the circumstances of her life. She would wait until Kelsey wanted to talk to her again, then be there to offer support and love. She would drive Gwen to the airport, and whatever was going to happen would happen. By the end of this, the streets might even look clear enough that she will be able to focus on her foundation.

When the painting was finished, Stella took a step back to admire it. That was something she rarely did, so when she felt the urge, she knew that it was a good one. No one was more critical of her work than herself, and usually, when she finished something, her eyes traveled straight to all the little imperfections that would drive her crazy until the painting sold, and sometimes even longer. She swore she'd had nightmares about poor shading jobs she'd done on some of her early works. Her phone vibrated in her pocket, which she assumed was a text, until it vibrated again, and she realized it was ringing.

"Hello?"

"Hey, Mom," Kelsey said, and Stella's stomach dropped.

"Are you okay?"

"Yeah, I am," she said. "A tree hit a power line near Mariah's house, so we don't have electricity right now."

Stella breathed a sigh of relief that her daughter wasn't hurt, but still, the fact that the storm was so severe there was worrying.

"You're safe, though, right? Are Mariah's parents home?"

"Her mom came home to make sure we weren't alone."

Ah, that explained it. Kelsey had been slightly afraid, and she'd wanted to hear her mother's voice, even though she was angry.

"I'm glad. Do you want me to come get you?" She

didn't dare tell Kelsey that would require walking back home in the storm. If she had to, she would do it in a heartbeat.

"No," Kelsey said curtly. After all, she was still angry. "I'm fine. I just wanted to let you know. I knew you'd, like, freak if you didn't hear from me."

Stella smiled despite herself. "Thank you. Stay safe. Let me know when the storm passes, and—"

"Call if I need anything. I know. Bye, Mom."

Stella felt a little lighter, like the storm was beginning to lift in more ways than one. As she looked out the window, she realized that while the sun wasn't yet shining, the curtains of rain had parted, and everything looked a little brighter. Things were going to start looking up. She could feel it in her bones. If they didn't begin to improve, she would make things better for herself.

Already, things were so much better than they had been at this time a few years ago. Stella couldn't help but wonder how her life had taken this direction. Jeff had been such a normal guy. They had had such a normal marriage. Their story was cute, or at least, she had always thought so, but not extraordinary.

Stella had met Jeff in high school, and she hadn't expected the relationship to last after high school. Stella was from Trussville, Alabama, and her parents had only recently moved to Atlanta for her father's job. When the company had offered him a job in Atlanta, complete with a hefty bonus for relocating, he'd jumped at the new opportunity. Though she hated to leave her home town, Stella had actually been excited about it. She'd always dreamed about living in a big city—that was, until she actually lived in one.

As a teenager, the lack of anything to do in her small suburb felt stifling, but when she got to Atlanta, the size had been almost suffocating. Still, she'd been nothing but excited to get started in her new school. Stella was blonde and pretty—not the typical theater nerd. Jeff had been on the baseball team, and she'd been surprised he even noticed her.

In her small town in Trussville, most people married their high school sweethearts just because there were precious few other options for anyone who wasn't planning on leaving for college, which was most people. Her school district hadn't been the best, and most people just went right into working, either because their parents owned businesses in town, or because they studied a trade. Very few teenagers left.

Stella had always told herself that she wouldn't marry anyone she was dating in high school. She'd decided those relationships were meant to help her grow into the person she wanted to be. She went on dates to decide what and who she did and didn't like, how she deserved to be treated. When she'd started dating Jeff, it had been casual at first, but after the homecoming dance, he'd asked her to go steady, and with so much pressure from their peers who had already voted them "cutest couple" in the yearbook, she'd accepted. Her parents had been so happy for her, and they liked him. They had met Jeff a few times, including when he had picked her up for the dance, and they'd forced the couple to pose for a million photos.

Then, her parents had passed so suddenly. She and Jeff had been dating for a few months, but he definitely wasn't emotionally mature enough to handle everything she was going through. For months, she was angry. Gwen had taken her in to stay with their small family, and Stella knew that she'd been difficult, even at the time. She was angry as soon as Jeff left her sight. It took her a long time to be able to get into a car again, and even longer to get behind the wheel. Jeff, doubtlessly with guidance from Gwen, had been there for her. Every time she felt afraid, Jeff promised he'd take care of her, and for years, he had.

As Stella thought about that time, she realized that this was the first time she'd recalled the good times with Jeff without any sense of longing. Her mind had been using the fact that they had been happy as evidence that she'd made a mistake getting a divorce but remembering it in this moment didn't make her feel that way. She was able to hold both the thought that she and Jeff had been in love and had some wonderful times that she wouldn't trade for anything and the fact that separation was the right thing for her.

She loved who he was and missed what they'd had, but she felt no romantic feelings about the person who had wronged her so, about the man who was sitting in a jail cell for selfishly throwing their lives away. Even if she did want to go back, it wouldn't be the same. It never could be. For the first time since everything had happened, the thought of having Jeff gone from her life forever filled her with a sense of peace that she'd made the right choice—not righteous anger, nor anxious doubt, but peace.

She built herself a life that she loved and a life full of people who loved her. Her daughter would be supported. Looking at her painting, Stella knew that she had the talent to make it in this crazy business even if there were setbacks. She wanted to stay.

# Chapter Seventeen

The next morning, Stella woke up early to drive Gwen to the airport. She'd stayed up late for a lot of reasons. One of them was the fact that Kelsey was still not home, and although she'd checked in after the storm blew over, Stella still wished she could see her. Another was because despite everything, she still sort of hoped that Gwen would come down the hall and decide that she forgave her for not going back to Jeff after all. The last reason, though certainly not the least, was because she'd never gotten used to sleeping on the darn couch, which still hurt her back.

Unfortunately, Gwen did not come wake her up to forgive her before she left. That wasn't surprising, but Stella had held out a little hope that it might be a possibility. Even if Gwen had, Stella didn't know what she would say. How could she tell her that she wanted a relationship with her mother-in-law, one that was separate from and not dependent upon a relationship with Jeff? Perhaps it was selfish to think she could have such a thing. Maybe Gwen viewed this as a test of her loyalty, and of course, that would always lie with her own son. Stella craved that maternal guidance in her life, but maybe she needed to come to terms with the fact that she wouldn't have it—couldn't have it. She supposed that she would have to try to smooth things over in the car. If she couldn't at least get the two of them on cordial speaking terms, they were in for a very uncomfortable and long ride.

Gwen did not let Stella help her with the luggage, though whether this was because she was angry or because she was stubborn was anyone's guess. She hauled her three suitcases and her large carry-on bag into Stella's car, filling both the trunk and the back seat with no room to spare.

"All right, Gwen," Stella said as she slammed the trunk shut, "are you ready to go?"

Gwen nodded. "Yes," she replied.

"Do you have your ID? Your ticket?"

"I do, both are in my bag."

Stella forced a smile. This was more than she'd talked to her mother-in-law in days, so she supposed she should be grateful, but instead, she felt disappointed. It was distressing for her to leave on such a bitter note. If things were to continue like this, Stella doubted very much that Gwen would keep up correspondence when she landed in Atlanta.

"Sounds good. Let's get going."

"Wait!"

Stella whipped around, confused at the sound of Kelsey's voice and noticed the car pulling up near the end of their driveway. Mariah was behind the wheel, and Kelsey was still in her pajamas, as if this had been such a last-minute decision that she hadn't even had the time to get dressed.

"Kelsey!" Gwen cried, elated. Kelsey had called Gwen the evening before and apologized for the fact that she wasn't going to be there to see her off to the airport despite Stella's scolding. Gwen had reassured her that she understood, that she deserved to take the space she needed from home if that was going to make her feel better, but Stella could tell that it had hurt. Kelsey was half the reason she'd even come to visit, so it was obviously going to hurt her feelings if she didn't properly say good-bye. Stella hadn't wanted to mention to Kelsey that it was perhaps the last time they would see Gwen if she remained angry about the divorce. Stella knew that if she told Kelsey that, she would change her mind about coming home to see her grandmother off to the airport.

Kelsey came bounding up the driveway, still looking half asleep, and gripped her grandmother in a tight hug that seemed to last forever.

"Sorry I almost missed you," she apologized, but Gwen shook her head.

"Nonsense," Gwen said, her eyes misty with joy. "I'm just glad you made it."

Stella smiled proudly. She felt a little guilty for even having assumed that Kelsey might not come home to see Gwen. Even as angry as she might have been with Stella, Kelsey made the right choices. She was a good kid even when she was upset. Sometimes she just needed a little time to arrive at the right decision.

"Hey, kid," she greeted when Kelsey looked her in the eyes. "I knew you'd come." That wasn't exactly true, but she liked to think that somewhere, in the back of her mind, she had believed that all along.

"I realized I was being a little unreasonable," she admitted. "We can talk about it later."

Stella couldn't wait. It was all she wanted. Kelsey and Gwen hugged and kissed good-bye, and Gwen said that she would visit again soon. Though that might have been a hollow promise she had no intention of following through on, Stella took it as a good sign.

"You know," Gwen said once they were in the car, driving down the street as Kelsey waved to them from the driveway, "you raised a really great kid."

Stella laughed. "Yeah," she agreed, "we really did."

There was a silence then but not an uncomfortable one. The pause was pregnant with anticipation, Gwen hoping that Stella would double back and tell her all the things she wanted to hear, and Stella hoping that she would not ask again.

"Jeff was always the disciplinarian," Stella admitted. "When he went away, I didn't think I was going to be able to fill that void. I wondered how in the world I was going to be able to raise Kelsey all by myself."

Gwen sighed. "It must have been hard," she said, "to have to do all that without him. It must have felt like he let you down."

"Mostly, I just felt guilty."

"For not having seen it coming?"

She shook her head. "For not being enough for him. I wondered why he'd needed more. Would he have done what he did if I'd gone back to work after Kelsey was born?

Or if I'd actually been successful in my art career back then?"

Gwen frowned. "It's not a matter of whether you were enough," she reasoned. "Not ever. He had a wonderful life, and he thought that what he did was going to make it even better for all of you."

"It didn't work out that way."

"I didn't say he was the sharpest tool in the shed." She laughed. It felt good to hear her laugh. "I mean, in some ways, he's one of the most brilliant people I know. In others, he's got to be one of the dumbest. I'm still reeling from it all."

"Me too," Stella said. She hesitated. "I hope you can understand, someday, why I can't take him back. I hope you know it's not because I didn't love him, or even that I ever stopped. It's just—"

"Trust," Gwen finished. "You can't trust him. I get it." Stella gripped the steering wheel so hard that her knuckles turned white. Gwen sounded annoyed again, and she cursed herself for bringing this up at all. Finally, Gwen let out a long, slow hiss of air from pursed lips. "I do get it. And I respect the choice you made, even if I don't agree with it."

Stella felt as though she could cry, but she blinked back the wetness from her eyes, worried that if she let the tears spill over, she'd lose sight of the road.

"Does that mean you'll call me when you get back to Atlanta?"

Gwen, for once, was speechless for a solid moment. "I'm sorry if I made you feel like my love for you is conditional," she said. "I was upset, and honestly, I still am, a bit. I think you're making a mistake, leaving your husband, the father of your child like that. Really, I think there will come a day when you wake up in your bed and regret your choice, and I just want you to be able to see that coming before it happens. I don't want you to get hurt twice."

Stella didn't argue. "In truth, I've wondered the same thing myself," she admitted. "But I think that I've reached a good place. I'm at peace. Where I am now, I'm not worried I'll have regrets because I really love the life I've made for myself. I might always wonder what Jeff and I could have had if I had taken him back, but I don't think I'll feel regret."

Gwen, though still unhappy, seemed to accept that. "I want you to have what you need in life, Stella," she said, and for the first time, Stella realized that she felt that she did. Even with everything that she'd lost—her lavish life-style, the house, so many friends, and her husband—she didn't feel like she wanted for anything. What was important was that she had her daughter, her passion, and love and support in her life from so many people. Nothing was missing.

Stella and Gwen managed some pleasant small talk for the rest of the drive, which was more than Stella had been expecting. Although Gwen had been staying in her home, Stella had missed her. It had been years since the two had gone more than a night or two without speaking. Stella tried to call most nights if only for a few minutes of conversation. Jeff was an only child after all, and Gwen wasn't married. She lived all alone, and Stella always worried about her, as independent as she was.

"She's your mother, Jeff," she had always nagged. "She needs someone to call her and make sure she's all right. You should be checking in with her more often." Jeff always agreed with her and promised that he would, but he rarely did, and Stella had always been the one to call at the end of the night and make sure Gwen had everything she needed. After the divorce, she'd felt that it was even more necessary than ever that someone make sure she was all right. Jeff going to prison had been so hard on her, and Stella worried about Gwen's heart. She was in good health, but having lost her own parents so suddenly, sometimes, Stella's anxieties would run wild.

The light conversation made the rest of the drive to the airport seem short, and it didn't take much time for them to get Gwen through airport security and check her baggage. Stella sat with Gwen in the lobby until they called to begin boarding her flight, and she stood.

"That's me, dear," she said when the announcement came through. Stella felt her eyes well up with tears. All this time, a part of her had been feeling a bit overwhelmed by the long visit, but now, she wasn't ready for it to be over.

"I don't want you to go," she admitted, and Gwen smiled, her own eyes dewy and sad. "You're so far away. When's the next time I'll see you?"

"Soon," she promised. "You'll have to come back to Atlanta to visit, okay? I'm getting too old to sit for these long flights."

Stella laughed. "Next time, Kelsey and I will come to you. Maybe for the holidays."

Gwen nodded, then pulled her in for a tight, long hug. It was interrupted by a second announcement from the speakers saying that the flight was ready for the economy class passengers, almost as if to urge them to hurry up and finish their good-byes.

"I love you, Stella. And Kelsey, too. I always will, no matter what happens. Be good, okay?"

Stella nodded. From the tone of their last conversation, she knew that Gwen still wasn't fully happy with where they'd landed on the Jeff situation, but Stella was glad to see that Gwen was meeting her halfway. That was all she could ask of her.

"Call me when you land and again when you get home, all right?"

Gwen agreed to do so, and Stella stood there waving until she disappeared down the long corridor to board the plane, looking back only once to smile at her.

# Chapter Eighteen

Stella had a long time to think on her drive back to Sunrise Beach. She'd brought a book on tape, which was playing something about Frida Kahlo through her speakers. As she listened to all the tragic losses that had befallen the Mexican painter, she couldn't help but think of how her own sadness had affected her art. Frida had taken up painting after a bus accident had broken her pelvis and spine, and she used her art as a way to express her constant, intense pain and all the things she couldn't articulate any other way. Her paintings were a glimpse into the mind of a young woman who had lost so much, and as Stella listened, she hoped to channel even half of that bravery.

More than anything, Frida was probably known, at least to Stella, for her self-portraits. She would paint herself exactly as she was even if she added a magical twist. In one oil painting Stella loved, she had painted herself with a broken Ionic column for a spine, signifying the pain she had endured after a failed surgery, and her unibrow, prominently displayed on her tear-stained face. She didn't hide her pain, nor did she view it as a flaw. These things were just allowed, in Frida's art, to be what they were.

As the narrator of the book droned on about Frida's tumultuous marriage, Stella vowed to be just like her in that sense. No longer would she force herself to imagine a more perfect version of her life, one in which she had never been hurt and was ashamed of her imperfections. If she wanted to succeed, in her art and in her life, she had to recognize the pain for what it was. The things she lost, the things she missed, were a part of her, and there would always be people who judged her for them. People who were insecure about their own lives often spent a lot of time judging those of other people—she knew that much from her gossipy ex-friend group in Atlanta. She knew for a fact that those women talked about her after the divorce, and as she thought about going back to that city to visit Gwen, she felt a little less dread than she normally did imagining the trip. Like Frida, she would find beauty in the way things were, not in the way she felt they should be or the way other people wanted them to be. The only way she was going to be able to move forward was to accept her life.

She pulled over for a cup of coffee when the dulcet tones of the narrator nearly put her to sleep, and eventually, she turned on the radio instead. That was something she rarely did, so it took her a while to search around for a station she liked, finally settling upon something that sounded much more like Kelsey's music tastes than her own. Modern pop, she thought with a grimace. What had happened to the rock she grew up with?

Finally, after what felt like forever, Stella arrived back home. The first thing she thought was that she might strip the sheets and throw them in the wash, so she could sleep in her own bed for the first time in weeks. That was going to be lovely.

"Hey," a voice called from the kitchen, and Stella, having thought she was home alone, yelped loudly. "Easy!" Kelsey laughed. "It's me."

"I thought you went back to Mariah's," Stella said, and Kelsey looked down at her feet sheepishly.

"I didn't. I'm back."

Stella nodded. "Any particular reason?"

"You're really going to make me say it, huh?" Kelsey asked, and Stella looked at her expectantly. "I was wrong. I shouldn't have run away like that just because I was mad at you." Stella hadn't thought of what Kelsey had done as running away, and the words made her feel a little nauseous.

"No, you shouldn't have."

"I just felt so betrayed," she continued. "Like, I lost all my friends when we moved. Sure, they weren't the best friends in the world, but they were mine, and we always had fun together. Then, I had to come here and make all new ones, and the second I did, it felt like they'd rather hang out with you than me."

"You realize that's ridiculous, right?" Stella almost smiled. "They weren't hanging out with me, Kels. I'm old. They're taking a class as a hobby. It's not personal."

"Well, it felt personal," Kelsey argued. "When Dani and Joey canceled on me, they literally just texted that they weren't going to make it because they were hanging out with you."

Stella blinked. "I think they might have been joking."

"Yeah, I know that now!" Kelsey said. "But in the moment, it just felt like I was being rejected, like they didn't want to stick around and be with me. And I thought maybe I wasn't fun enough or smart enough or whatever. They clearly liked you better."

Oh, Stella thought. Maybe this went a little deeper than just being bitter about a boring Saturday afternoon with nothing to do.

"There's nothing you're not smart enough for," Stella reassured, "and they certainly weren't sticking around to clean paint brushes because it was more fun than being with you. They had questions about a career in art. That's all."

"I know. I overreacted, and I really shouldn't have left. I'm sorry."

Stella smiled. "I'm just glad you're back. I love you."

Kelsey rolled her eyes as Stella pulled her into a tight hug. "Love you too, Mom."

For lunch, Stella decided to take Kelsey out rather than just having her eat a sandwich at home like she normally did. Kelsey was growing up after all, and it was worth spending some time with her out of the house. It had been a long time since the two of them had gone out and just talked since Kelsey spent most of her time in her room studying, and Stella was often out running errands for her classes. Having Gwen around made Stella realize just how much she missed it, as Kelsey told stories about school that she'd never told before around the dinner table and mentioned friends Stella had never met. It had drawn attention to the fact that even though things had been agreeable, she'd fallen out of touch with her daughter a little, and she was determined to get back in sync.

A few days passed and things were beginning to go back to normal. Stella was enjoying sleeping in her own bed, of course, and Gwen had called her to say that she'd arrived home safely and that there had been no issues with her flight. Since then, they hadn't spoken every night, like they normally did, but Gwen certainly hadn't written Stella out of her life, and that was good enough. They still chatted every other night or so, and when they did, Gwen seemed to be in relatively good spirits. Sure, she talked more often about how she visited Jeff in prison and how she really believed that he was turning things around for himself, but she was no longer pushing for Stella to take him back. If she were being honest, Stella had gotten to a place where she could almost be happy for Jeff. Part of her still cared for him, after all, and probably always would. As much as she still felt angry and hoped that he paid for what he had done to their family, prison and a divorce were enough of a punishment. When Gwen told Stella that he'd been getting involved in some community outreach and mentoring other prisoners about business, since he did have an MBA despite his poor choices, she was glad to hear it. He'd suffered enough, and it was a good thing that he was apparently seeing the light.

In the daytime, Stella was laser-focused like she'd never been before. With the success of her first class, she had found that even more perspective students were interested in taking a course. Kelsey's friends, after a long heart to heart between the three of them at school, had come back to the class with Kelsey's blessing. Almost all of Stella's current students were interested in taking a second course that was more advanced. When she wasn't painting her own works, she was planning a curriculum for her next course and getting together the materials she'd need to offer a second round of beginner classes. She even started watching free videos about website design and had nearly overhauled her site to allow students to sign up online rather than having to email her. When she'd figured out how to add a calendar to her webpage, she'd been so excited she'd rushed in to show Kelsey, who had been less than impressed but managed some half-convincing fake praise.

"I'm proud of you, Mom," she'd said. "I didn't know you had it in you."

She got the feeling Kelsey might be talking about more than just the website. Everything was going swimmingly, and for the first time in a long time, Stella was proud of herself, too.

Of course, undercutting that confidence was a sense of shame that reared its ugly head every time she thought about Maisie. How could Stella have been so naive? She had given her paintings, several really good ones, to someone she barely even knew on the promise that she would sell them and give Stella the majority of the profits. It had sounded too good to be true, and she shouldn't have believed it in the first place. She lamented this into her tea at the Townsend Cafe, and Felicia shook her head.

"Stella, darling, you're so hard on yourself. It's not your fault. Someone lied to you. How, exactly, were you in the wrong there?"

"I shouldn't have believed it."

"What were you supposed to do, give the woman a background check? You'd been corresponding for weeks, and then when she showed up, she was exactly who she said she was. She sent you her website and everything, and it looked so official. She had me fooled."

"But we were able to find out that the other paintings weren't hers so easily," Stella pointed out.

"Easily?" Felicia exclaimed. "You practically became a private detective overnight! It's an understandable mistake. Anyone could have made it."

Stella didn't argue, knowing that Felicia would keep fighting with her until she finally succumbed to the opinion that it wasn't her fault, but it didn't completely quell the doubts in her mind. At the end of the day, she had willingly handed her paintings to a thief, and that made this feel so much worse than if someone had just broken into the gallery and stolen them. That, she thought, she could live with, but this was driving her crazy.

"How has it been seeing your brother again? I know it's been a few months since you were last able to do that."

Felicia's face lit up. She and Stella hadn't been able to see one another much between Stella's busy schedule and Felicia spending her lunches helping Graham settle in. "It's been wonderful to have him back." Stella smiled.

"I can't wait to meet him. When do you think he might be free to have dinner with the two of us?"

"Oh, any time!" Felicia said which surprised Stella. Felicia had been saying that Graham's schedule had been so busy with virtual meetings and reports for the business with which he was consulting, so it was a little strange to hear that he was suddenly so free.

"Has he finished his work or something?"

"To be perfectly honest, he really only works an 8 to 5 day," she admitted. "I just wanted to wait until your mother-in-law left to introduce the two of you. I thought she might be a bit of a downer for any chemistry that might spark between you."

Stella laughed and smacked her on the arm playfully. "There's not going to be any chemistry!" she maintained, something she'd been trying to tell Felicia since the moment she announced that he was coming into town. "I'm not looking for chemistry. I've had it, and it's great, but now I'm just trying to focus on my career."

"I'm not saying you're *looking* for it," Felicia said, "but that's the perfect time to find it, don't you think?" When Stella gave her nothing but an incredulous look, Felicia sighed. "Trust me. I'm something of a matchmaker, and I can tell when people are going to hit it off."

Stella still couldn't find herself believing that in a romantic sense, but she shrugged anyway, taking a long sip of her tea. Suddenly, she felt her phone buzz in her pocket. Assuming it was Kelsey calling to ask if she could borrow the car, she answered without looking.

"Hello?"

"Stella, hi," a familiar voice said, and Stella froze. Apparently, the shock was clear on her face because Felicia set down her mug, leaning forward in concern. Stella waved her off to let her know that nothing horrendous had happened.

"Maisie?" she asked. She felt her face flush, and her

heart started to race uncomfortably in her chest. How could this woman have the audacity to call her after running out with her paintings and not getting in touch with her for weeks? Did she really think Stella was so stupid as to make the same mistake again and ship her more art even after what had happened?

"I'm so sorry I haven't been in contact with you," Maisie said. "I dropped my phone at the airport, and it shattered. It's taken me forever to relocate all my contacts."

"I left you messages."

"Yeah, I had a bit of a family emergency, too. My mom fell, so I took a bit of unplanned time off work. I'm sorry about that."

Now, Stella felt guilty but still a bit suspicious. She wasn't letting her guard down so easily this time. "I'm so sorry to hear that. Is she all right?"

"She's doing much better now, but the fall scared her pretty badly. She decided she wanted to move to assisted living, so my brothers and I have been getting her settled, visiting a lot to make sure she doesn't get lonely. It's been kind of nice to have family around, honestly."

Stella knew the feeling, but still didn't cave. Maisie had known that Gwen was visiting, so she could easily be trying to win her sympathy. She waited for Maisie to continue.

"Anyway, I wanted to tell you that your paintings sold like hotcakes. Seriously, it's been a long time since I've had art move like that. It was amazing! You're really talented, you know."

For a long moment, Stella was shocked speechless. "What?" she asked. "You sold them?"

Maisie laughed. "Well, yeah. What did you think I was

going to do with them?" Stella didn't want to reply to that, suddenly feeling embarrassed. Had she really been so wrong about this?

"I checked out your website," she blurted, regretting the statement instantly. Maisie paused.

"Yes? Did you have a question about it?"

Stella took a deep, steadying breath and told herself to be brave. She was entitled to some answers. "Well, when I didn't hear from you, I started to worry that maybe... Well, my daughter taught me to search for the source of an image, and I tried it with a few of your paintings. They were all done by different artists."

To Stella's surprise, Maisie chuckled. "Oh!" she exclaimed. "Yes, there was an HTML problem with the site for a few weeks, but it should be fixed now if you check back. It's supposed to bring you to the artist's portfolio online if you click on the images. I was going to ask you if you were interested in having your paintings listed there, too."

Stella couldn't believe what she was hearing. "Wait, so they're... all posted with permission from the artists?"

"Of course. They're my clients. Only the last few paintings on the site are mine since I try to give most of the space to my artists who need it. The artists who don't paint on commission or have other sources of income are listed first, so you'd be a little further down on the page since you've got your classes. I still think it could drum up a little bit of business for you, especially if you'd be willing to start shipping your art to perspective buyers. It's totally up to you, though."

Confusion gave way to guilt as the pieces fell together.

Maisie hadn't been telling her that the entire site was her paintings, just that they were her painters. Maisie hadn't been stealing her art at all, and that meant that it had really sold, just like she'd said it would. Stella's own artwork had been sold by a professional art saleswoman to real collectors. Most of the works she'd sold had gone into offices or the living rooms of her friends and family. Now, it was being looked at by professionals in the field, and they liked it, many wanted to buy it.

"I would love that," Stella agreed when she was finally able to form words through all the happy, racing thoughts. A minute ago, she'd thought she was down a few thousand dollars, and now, she'd turned a profit.

"The paintings sold for a really decent amount, too," Maisie continued, as if Stella's jaw wasn't already on the floor just from hearing that Maisie had sold them at all. "I brought two of them to an auction, and one made almost a thousand, while the other was a little over. That's pretty impressive for a beginner, someone who has never done an auction before and whose name isn't known at all."

"Two thousand dollars?" Stella verified, feeling as though she were floating. That was more than double what she charged here in the gallery. People around here wouldn't, couldn't buy art for that kind of a price.

"And that's just the two I brought to the auction with me. Afterward, I told a few of the people who'd been outbid on your art that I had a few others, and they practically came running. All in all, that kind of attention is something a lot of artists spend their whole careers searching for, and you didn't even have to advertise yourself. It's amazing."

While Maisie began the breakdown of her funds, how much Stella would make off the sales, and how Maisie would get the money to her, she zoned out a bit, letting her mind wander. She hadn't had her art stolen after all. While she still felt a little guilty for having assumed the worst, Felicia had done the same, and it had made sense. The circumstances had been so crazy that she didn't know what else she could have thought. After having the nitty gritty explained to her, she thanked Maisie for everything and hung up the phone. She turned her attention back to Felicia, who hadn't even been politely pretending not to eavesdrop.

"Was that the artist?" she asked, and Stella nodded.

"Apparently it was a misunderstanding," she said. "She sold the paintings, and she's going to send me the money soon. They sold for a lot."

Felicia grinned. "That's amazing, Stella!" she exclaimed, and Stella finally felt the shock wear off and the joy spread through her, warming her from the chest out.

"My paintings sold!" she reiterated, beaming, and she and Felicia held hands for a quiet, squealing celebration.

"We must celebrate!" Felicia decided. "We'll have dinner, all of us. You, me, and your daughter."

"What about Graham?"

She winked. "I'm still hoping that your first meeting will be solo," she said, and Stella rolled her eyes, too happy to be properly annoyed. "Start thinking of places you want to eat. Dinner is on me, so pick something extravagant!"

The celebration idea made Stella smile. Gwen had taken her to the uptown seafood place to celebrate the success of her classes. But besides that, it had been a long time since she'd celebrated accomplishments with people she cared about. The last time she could remember was her high school graduation when her aunt came to visit from Alabama to take her to one of the fanciest steakhouses in Atlanta. She must have saved for weeks to be able to afford the overpriced dinner, but it was one of the nicest meals Stella ever had in her life, at least at the time. Years later, with his wealth, Jeff would take her to places like that all the time, but it never meant as much as that one dinner with her aunt.

They celebrated Jeff's accomplishments all the time. When he got his first job at a big company, when he was promoted, when he got his astronomical raise...

Kelsey, too. Stella always made sure to schedule a fancy dinner or some nice vacation after Kelsey returned straight A's for a semester, passed her final exams with flying colors, or received any kind of award at school, even if it was just perfect attendance or something else that Kelsey swore wasn't worth making a big deal over. Stella wanted to make sure Kelsey always felt valued, and at that time, they did so with monetary spoils as well as spending time together. Now, as she had only the latter to give, she realized that the former was almost irrelevant.

Still, she wasn't about to turn down a free steak dinner with her best friend and her daughter. Kelsey would love it.

# Chapter Nineteen

As Stella's new students filed into her studio, she couldn't keep the grin from her face. The class was almost twice the size of her first, so she'd cleared out some of the boxes and other things in the back area she was using for storage to give the class space more room. The first class she had offered had just been a trial run. She hadn't wanted to spend a whole lot of time and energy on converting the studio, if she wasn't going to use it for this purpose again, but she had been convinced to offer two classes this time around. This was the first meeting of the beginners, and while most looked excited, one or two seemed a bit nervous, and she was hoping that a calm, happy greeting would be enough to put them at ease.

"Okay, everybody," she announced, "I see some familiar faces and some new ones. I'm glad you're all here. We're going to have a lot of fun over the next few weeks, and I hope you'll all learn a lot. Who here has painting experience?" The two students that had already taken Stella's first beginner class raised their hands tentatively, as did one other, but the rest looked a little overwhelmed. Stella smiled. "That's okay. This is a beginner class, and there's no experience necessary, I promise. I just wanted to get a feel for where we are. Did everyone bring a book to paint? If not, I have a few, just in case."

All the students pulled books out of their bags and purses, setting them on the long table Stella had prepared for this purpose. She'd decorated it with things like plastic flowers and a white tablecloth to provide a nice backdrop.

"The flowers are optional. Since I know a few of you have been here before, I figured you might want something a little more exciting than just the book, so you can add in the background, too. If you're new, you're welcome to try, but if you don't feel like you want to just yet then it's fine to focus only on your book."

"Oh, thank goodness," a little old man named Herbert exclaimed, and a few of the others laughed. "I thought I was going to have to paint the whole garden!"

Stella chuckled. "No, of course not. I'm never going to ask you to do anything crazy that you're not ready for."

"Is my book too thin?" a young girl asked. Her name was Claudia, and she was only eleven. Stella had been a little hesitant about teaching someone so young in a classroom full of people who were much older than her, fearing that she might feel intimidated. But her father had said that it was something she wanted to do and had even signed up to take the class with her, so Stella couldn't say no. It was too sweet, and she wasn't going to get in the way of some adorable family bonding.

"Your book is perfect, Claudia." She turned back to address the room. "The goal here is to get a feel for straight lines, curves, and shadows. We'll also look a little bit at how different colors play together. It's okay if it doesn't look perfect, and you won't finish in this one session. We spend a few sessions dedicated to each project, and if you're not ready to move on when the rest of the class does, I can accommodate that, too. This is about you finding out what you like to paint, and it should always be fun."

There was a small murmur of agreement as a few of the students who knew one another turned to chat. Stella instructed them to begin sketching the base of the painting with charcoal, so they would know where they wanted to place each color later. She turned on the radio at a low volume and walked around slowly, answering questions as she went and giving praise as often as she could.

It had surprised her just how natural she found teaching. The process brought her back to when Kelsey was young, and Stella would help with her homework. Kelsey had found history to be particularly difficult, as she could never remember names and dates. They all jumbled in her mind, and Stella's whip-quick, brilliant young daughter had never done well when a subject didn't come naturally to her. As a child, she quickly got frustrated and gave up on herself since she was used to everything being easy for her in school. Stella remembered sitting in Kelsey's room so many times while she cried over a B- she'd gotten on a test. She was so accustomed to straight A's, and Stella reassured her that life was about more than just grades, that everyone had things that were difficult for them, and that she was still proud of Kelsey no matter what. She found herself falling back into a similar pattern of reassurances for her students. "Things like this take time," she would say. "You're using a skill you've never used before. It's like flexing a muscle. You'll get better at it the more you do it."

Part of the reason she liked teaching so much, she thought, was because she missed that nurturing, comforting part of herself. Now that Kelsey was grown, Stella rarely had to do that anymore. Kelsey soothed herself when she was upset. She didn't tell Stella about every grade that was lower than she'd hoped or every test that was harder than she'd expected. It was a good thing, Stella knew. It meant that she'd taught Kelsey the skills to be able to calm herself down about disappointments like these before they spiraled into full-blown anxiety attacks. That didn't stop her from sometimes missing feeling needed.

Stella's second class was a more advanced beginner class. She had struggled with the wording on the website for a while.

"It's not quite intermediate," she had told Felicia, "but it's not beginner, either. It's in the middle."

Settling for "advanced beginner" and hoping that everyone would understand, she had started receiving sign up requests quickly. Before she knew it, the whole class had filled up. It wasn't just her students from the first class that wanted to move on, but also a few people who had either taken painting classes elsewhere in the past or were self-taught and had been painting for a while. As a result, the class had a lot more variety in skill level with some people having learned the basics a few weeks ago and others having been painting for years. Still, the atmosphere of the class was so welcoming and inviting that she hadn't had anyone complain or ask to be moved to a lower class, so she hoped she was doing a good job of leveling the playing field. She gave the more advanced painters more intricate background details to practice while focusing on the foreground for her less experienced, and it seemed to be working.

Joey and Dani had signed up, too. They'd tried to convince Kelsey to take the beginner class, and Stella had told her that of course, if she wanted to, she wouldn't have to pay, but Kelsey hadn't been interested. It was expected, Stella thought. Kelsey had always been more like her father in that way, not interested in the arts.

One day, a few weeks into the class, she caught Dani staring at her canvas rather than painting. Stella frowned and came up behind her gently.

"Something on your mind?" she asked, and Dani shook her head to snap herself out of her daze.

"Oh!" she exclaimed. "Sorry, it's nothing. I was just thinking."

Stella smiled patiently. "Thinking about what?"

"Well, you were telling Joey and me about that exhibit you did a few months back," she began. "And I was just thinking about how I wished we could do something like that."

Stella blinked. "You mean an art exhibit? With your paintings?"

"Yeah!" Dani chirped, then hesitated. "But, like, not just mine. I'm not that good, and I've only got a few finished paintings. I mean all of us, all the students, and you, too!"

It hadn't occurred to Stella that her students might want to sell their art, but it made sense. She had assumed that they'd wanted to keep everything they had painted, but perhaps she had been wrong. After all, most of their paintings were things she instructed them to paint rather than their own choice, and while she gave them a lot of freedom to decide what they might want to paint within each category—still life, landscapes, portraits, etc.—they didn't necessarily feel attached to all of them. Maybe an exhibit would be fun. Not to mention, it would give the younger college students a taste of what it was like to be a professional artist. While the exhibit had been a blast on the actual night, the work leading up to it had been brutal. It would be a realistic glimpse into the blood, sweat, and tears behind the glamor.

"That sounds like a really great idea, Dani," she agreed. "We can start organizing it, and maybe at the end of the class in a couple of weeks, we'll have a big exhibit featuring everyone's work who wants to participate."

Dani brightened, looking both excited and praised, and her elated face made Stella feel warm inside. She'd come to care for some of these kids like her own, and she wanted to give them every opportunity she could.

As her students sketched copies of their favorite books, Stella thought about the exhibit. In between answering questions and giving instructions, she was daydreaming about bragging about her students and watching them make money off their art. Something like this might have changed her own opinion about painting if she'd been a part of it.

She'd viewed her art as a hobby for all these years, never believing that she could do anything worthwhile with it.

Stella had taken a few classes at the community college in Atlanta, but that hadn't been aimed toward people who were serious about an art career. In fact, the possibility of making an income by selling paintings had never even come up in that class, and she had thought it was just an unrealistic dream to imagine that anyone might want to display her art in their homes. Now that it was her reality, she hoped to spread that wealth and let these excited kids know that, while it was a lot of work, it was possible.

Teaching three classes a week was exhausting but rewarding. Her advanced beginners painted on both Mondays and Fridays, while her beginner newbies only met on Wednesdays. In between those days, Stella was prepping for her lessons, organizing and cleaning the studio, and managing the gallery. She barely found the time to paint for herself anymore, and while she loved what she was doing, she found that she missed it.

Lately, she'd been staying up late to paint since it was the only time she had to herself. She might be losing some sleep, but it was worth it, in her mind, to be able to continue her passion. Besides, if she didn't practice, she could lose all the skills she'd been working so hard to teach. Not to mention that paintings from her gallery were still selling at a steady, if not altogether rapid, rate. She sold a few a month, which meant that she needed to replace them at that rate, and that was becoming increasingly demanding to keep up with.

Because of that, Stella decided to close her shop on Tuesdays, so she could dedicate the entire day to painting. She didn't even go to the studio, where she had been doing most of her paintings lately. Instead, Stella decided to load her paints and easel into her car and find a new, fresh location to paint—something she hadn't already done before.

As soon as she started the car, she realized that she had no idea where she was going. She hadn't exactly done a lot of sightseeing, even though she'd already been living there for so long. Most days, she went to the same few places— her gallery, the grocery store, a few shops around town, the beach, and home. She had a doctor and a dentist, but she visited neither more than once every six months or so. She jogged the same path nearly every day, as she liked to be out early and wanted to ensure she was running along a populated trail where she wouldn't be alone, for safety. It was rare for her to see a new sight. Perhaps that was just how it was in small towns, she thought.

She drove aimlessly for a while, allowing the car to take her wherever it wanted. She made turns at random, hoping to find herself somewhere unfamiliar and new, but when she finally put her car into park, she found that she had autopiloted to somewhere even better.

Stella dragged her bag of paints and her easel to the front of the Townsend Cafe, setting her things up in front of one of the outdoor seats. She had never thought to paint here before, but it made sense. Felicia's aesthetic was immaculate—everything from the plants she kept around the shop and at every table to the beautiful, delicate teacups to the perfectly petite little madeleines dipped in dark chocolate.

"Stella," the waitress, Juana, greeted. "I'm surprised to see you sitting outside. Is Felicia meeting you?"

Stella shook her head. "No, I actually came on my own today. I want to paint something here."

Juana looked a little confused. Stella had chatted with Juana a few times, but nothing very in-depth, and she was fairly certain they'd never gotten into what Stella did for a living. "Oh!" she confirmed the hunch with her surprise. "I didn't know you painted! That's so cool. My sister does, too. She's taking classes."

"Wait, what's your sister's name?"

"Maria," she replied, and Stella grinned.

"That's my class! I know her. She's lovely."

Juana rolled her eyes. "Yeah, when she's not borrowing your skirts and spilling juice on them," she laughed. "I had no idea. She really loves your class. Every time she comes home on Wednesdays, she's talking about how much fun she had. She almost had me convinced to sign up. Now that I know it's you teaching, maybe I will!"

Stella smiled, then placed her order when Juana asked. She never really ordered pastries, but the cherry cheese danish was beautiful, and she wanted to paint that. It was shiny from a drizzle of honey and lightly speckled with icing sugar that looked like snow on top of the dark, fresh cherry preserves Felicia made in-house. Stella had been eyeing it for months but had never actually ordered it It was a bit too big for one person to finish, in her opinion, and Felicia was a type 1 diabetic and didn't eat sweets often.

"I'll find you the prettiest one," Juana promised before heading off to retrieve the order. Stella looked out over the terrace wondering why she never sat outside when she and

Felicia had lunch. It was nice, beautiful even though the parking lot was only feet away.

She waited for her pastry to arrive, and when it did, she painted it. When Juana noticed that she wasn't eating it, she brought her a cookie to nibble on while the pastry served as a model. Stella wasn't sure how long she sat there painting, but by the time she was finally done, it was late in the afternoon, so it must have been hours.

"Juana," she called, "I brought my plates inside. Figured I'd save you the trip."

"There she is!" Felicia announced from the back. "The big ar*tiste!*" Stella laughed.

"Oh, hush. Sorry for using your storefront as a studio today. I thought I'd be finished faster than I was."

"It's no problem!" Felicia reassured. "I'd like to see the painting, if possible."

"Do you want a bag for the cherry danish?" Juana asked as she took the empty plate and teacup. Stella almost said no, but then nodded. Kelsey would eat it.

After having the pastry bagged, Stella led Felicia outside to see her art. She had been working more on perspective, so this painting was a little different than her normal. It looked like it was painted from her point of view sitting at the table rather than just a close up of the pastry, and she was proud of how it had turned out. It was always a gamble painting outside living near the coast, where the weather was always changing and unpredictable. More than once, she had gotten halfway through a painting and had to pack it up because grey clouds rolled in. A few times, she'd been too wrapped up in her art to notice and had her canvas ruined by rain. This one had turned out well, however, and the sun was still shining through the clouds. Though the sky wasn't clear, the clouds seemed light and fluffy like they were made of air rather than water, and she knew that they would not bring a storm with them.

"Stella," Felicia gasped, "it's gorgeous. Can I buy it?"

Stella blushed. "You don't have to buy it just because it's a painting of your cafe, Felicia. I promise I'm not offended."

"I'm being serious. How much?" Stella rolled her eyes jovially. Felicia was always supportive of her art but had never actually asked to put a piece in her cafe. She had a carefully curated design pattern inside, and most of Stella's paintings didn't fit with that. This one was no exception. The style of the cafe was very English, like a royal tearoom. When Stella sat at the very back booth like she always did, she felt as though she were waiting on the Queen to sit across from her.

"If you really like it, then consider it a gift."

"I couldn't!"

Stella smiled. "You never let me pay for my tea and lunches here. I owe you. It has to dry for a few days, and then I'll have to varnish it. After that, though, it's all yours."

Felicia looked delighted. "Thank you so much. I truly love it. It's gorgeous."

That was all Stella wanted, in the end. To have her paintings go to people who liked them, people who felt happy when they looked at them. She didn't care about notoriety or fame or even the money really, though she had to pay her income some mind because the bills didn't pay themselves. She wasn't looking to become rich from her art. She'd already had riches, and it hadn't made her happy, no matter how much Jeff had been convinced that it was the best thing for all of them. What she wanted was to feel fulfilled, and seeing Felicia's smiling face, made so happy by the painting of her shop, filled Stella with joy. She felt whole, complete, and like she was doing what she was meant to do in the world.

# Chapter Twenty

The following morning, Stella was in her gallery. She'd been neglecting some of the more banal chores around the place, like mopping and dusting, and it was beginning to show. Neglecting chores when she was excited about something else was one of her bad habits. She found herself thinking in every waking minute about the exhibit that she was going to put on with her students, and in what little time she spent not planning for that, she was painting. The sand that customers were tracking in on the bottoms of their feet was beginning to turn the linoleum a different color, and she knew that she needed to do something about it.

As she mopped, she couldn't stop thinking about the exhibit. If it were possible, she was even more eager for this one than she had been for her own months back. The exhibit she'd planned with Adelle had been fun at first, but as soon as Adelle had canceled, it had turned into a nightmare. Stella had barely managed to pull everything together after going back and forth on whether she would even go through with a show like that without a partner. The fear of her name and, by extension, Jeff's, was so loud in her ears that she had hardly even been able to enjoy the party. Afterward, her only regret had been that she'd let her fear get in the way so much, and she was determined not to do that this time.

Every detail had to be perfect. She would let the students vote on the snacks and beverages to ensure that everyone had something they liked and could eat. Their friends and family would be invited, of course. Maybe she would even go out and buy special stationary to give the families of her students a more inviting welcome. Of course, it would be a black-tie event, very formal and classy, but not intimidating. These were students after all. She wanted to make sure they felt valued, not intimidated. Above everything else, she wanted to make sure that it was a positive experience for everyone.

She was sure that Dani and Joey, and probably a few of Kelsey's other young friends from the art program, would be able to sell a few pieces. Their art was much farther along than most of her other students, and she usually had them working on a project that was several steps more advanced than everyone else in the class. Some of their paintings even looked like they could have been done by a professional. Joey liked to paint abstract, and Dani liked portraits of animals. Stella could see both of those things selling extremely well, especially since there had been no similar events in the area since her own show. With everything she'd learned from throwing the first exhibit, she was sure she could get her advertising to reach even farther than it had the first time. She even had a few friends at the news station because of her show that she was sure she could reach out to for some coverage.

Stella was so wrapped up in her thoughts that she didn't even hear the doorbell jingle with the arrival of a customer until she very nearly swept the mop over his patent leather shoes. She jumped back in shock and humiliation.

"I'm so sorry!" she exclaimed, covering her mouth with one hand. "I have no idea how I didn't see you there." She followed the shoes up a well-dressed man wearing grey slacks and a button-down, short-sleeved shirt. His beard was short and well-kept, and although Stella normally wasn't a huge fan of facial hair, it worked on this man. His black hair was short and slicked back, and he smiled at her. The corners of his light brown eyes crinkled.

"That's quite all right," he replied, and Stella knew immediately who he was based on his British accent that matched her friend's.

"You're Graham Townsend," she guessed, and he smiled.

"What gave it away?"

"We don't get a lot of Brits here," she replied. "Not to mention, you two look alike."

Graham frowned, but it was good natured. "Don't let Felicia hear you saying that," he said seriously. "She'll throw a fit. She's always hated when people point it out."

Stella blinked. "Why?"

"Probably because I look exactly like our father."

Stella couldn't help but laugh. "I'm Stella Britton," she greeted, extending her hand. Graham took it, and after he shook it, gently but firmly, he leaned in and placed a chaste kiss on either cheek. Felicia did that often, too, but when Graham did it, it made her heart skip in her chest.

"Can I, um, help you find something?" Stella asked, trying to cover up the fact that she was feeling so flustered. She hoped he didn't notice, but the glimmer of teasing in his eyes when he shook his head told her that she probably had no such luck.

"I'm just looking for now," he said. "Though I do have a few questions about the art. You're good. All these are your original designs?"

She nodded. "Yes. Most of them are from the past year or so, but a few are much older. I moved from Atlanta, Georgia, and I had painted a lot there, too." She wasn't sure why she was telling him all that, but she felt as though she couldn't make her mouth stop. Graham didn't look bothered, though. He nodded patiently, like he was hanging onto every word.

"Oh?" he asked. "That's a rather far journey. What brought you here to the beach?"

She shrugged. "A divorce, if I'm being honest."

Graham grimaced. "I'm so sorry."

"It's okay. It was for the best anyway." She was sure of that now and felt no guilt or shame when she told it to Graham. He nodded.

"It usually is, I find. Even the messiest of divorces happened for a reason, right? No use staying in a relationship that's making no one happy."

Stella smiled. It was refreshing to hear someone say that to her. Most of the time, when she told people about the divorce, she was met with pity or unwanted advice. Though she knew people meant well, sometimes it was hard for them to mind their own business. When it came to divorce, people often felt that their opinions would be helpful to her, even though they rarely were.

"My sister told me that you were an artist, but I had no idea you were so talented. I'm very impressed."

"Do you paint?" she asked, and he laughed.

"Oh, absolutely not. I'm awful at art. I can hardly draw a stick figure."

Stella couldn't help but laugh along. "I'm sure you're not as bad as you think. Anyone can learn to draw if they want to."

He shrugs. "I suppose that's been my problem," he admitted. "I'm a bit lazy in the artistic sense. When things don't look the way I've envisioned them in my head, I give up. I tried taking a pottery class when I was in college. I wanted to make a vase for my mother for Mother's Day. I worked so hard. I used the wheel and everything, spent hours spinning and massaging the clay until my hands fell asleep."

"And? How did it turn out?"

"Lumpier than spoiled milk!"

Both of them dissolved into laughter, and Stella found herself inching closer to Graham, wanting to talk to him more. She knew that she was busy, that the floor wasn't going to mop itself, but she was entranced. He was charming and funny, just like Felicia had said. Stella had been sure she was just trying to talk him up, so Stella would agree to a blind date, but Felicia was right. He seemed like a nice guy, and she wanted to know more about him. As much as she wanted to ask him to coffee, a more sensical voice inside told her that was a terrible idea. She could feel the butterflies beginning to flutter around in her stomach, and that wasn't a good sign. She couldn't have that, not with someone who didn't even live in her new hometown and certainly not so soon after her divorce.

It had been well over three years, sure, but the marriage was decades long. She was still grieving, and more than that, she was still working on picking up the pieces of her previous life and trying to make something new for herself and her daughter. She'd gotten this far by putting her nose to the grind and making things happen, and she couldn't lose focus now that she was so close to being where she wanted to be.

Where did she want to be? She wanted to be a successful artist for sure. Her own gallery, maybe a few more well-populated classes. Eventually, she thought she'd expand her studio into another building, perhaps uptown, where the college was. Most of the students lived in that part of town, and if she could afford a big space up there, she might have a large clientele from Kelsey's school alone.

Speaking of Kelsey, she wanted a relationship with her daughter that wasn't so hot and cold. Right now, Stella felt like she was walking on eggshells half the time, trying to enforce what was best while also letting Kelsey grow up and have freedom. Stella wanted Kelsey to understand where she was coming from in her decisions while also wanting to allow her daughter to feel her grief about her father being in prison. Things were tender right now, precariously balanced. One day, she and Kelsey were doing wonderfully, able to have lunch and see a movie together and laugh about silly old jokes. The next, Kelsey didn't even want to come home to live in the same house, staying at friends' places instead. Stella needed to patch that all up before she was able to think about anything else at all.

"You know," Graham said, interrupting her thoughts, "I'm really not in town often. I'm hoping that when my contract with the business I'm currently working for ends, that I'll have a little more freedom to visit. But right now, I'm not here nearly as frequently as I'd like."

Stella wasn't sure where he was going with that thought, but she nodded. "Yeah, Felicia has mentioned that to me. She misses you like crazy."

"I miss her, too," he admitted, "but don't ever tell her I've said that. It'll go straight to her head."

Stella laughed. Felicia certainly already knew how much he cared for her. He didn't seem like the type to hide his feelings for no reason. The two of them had just met, and he was already telling her some fairly personal things, if she did say so herself.

Of course, maybe he just felt bad for accidentally asking about her divorce. "She told me that you used to live here."

"Yes, years ago," he agreed. "As much as I love the traveling, I miss having a home base sometimes. It gets lonely, you know?"

Stella certainly did. "I get that. It's hard not to know

many people in an area. When I moved here, I thought I was going to lose my mind even though everyone was so nice and welcoming to me. I couldn't imagine relocating for my job every few years."

"It doesn't happen as frequently as you'd think," he corrected, "but when it does, it is difficult. It's a strain, socially. You meet new people and have to immediately leave them behind."

"Why is it so hard to make friends as an adult?" Stella asked. "My daughter is in college, and she brings home a new friend once a week. Here I am, trying my hardest just to keep up with saying hello to the neighbors often enough that they don't start to wonder if they need to report me missing."

He laughed. "I completely agree. Meeting people is hard." He took a long, meaningful pause, turning to Stella slowly in a way that made her shiver slightly. He seemed so nice and having his full attention felt wonderful. "But I do think I've enjoyed meeting you."

Stella couldn't lie. The truth was always written all over her face. "Likewise."

Graham leaned in and kissed her on the cheeks once again. "I hope we can meet again soon, Stella Britton."

As Graham left, Stella was left alone with her thoughts, and the only thing she could think about was that she might be in trouble.

But for now, she'd just relax and enjoy the moment. The rush of excitement that a handsome man showed interest in her was so very nice. She'd missed that... at least a little.

Smiling, she snuggled into the couch and tucked her

feet up under her. Yes, she'd remember this night for a while.

———

Want to know what happens next in Stella's journey? Grab Book 3, *Living for Today*. Here's a little about it:

Stella Britton continues to build a new life for her and her teenage daughter in the cozy beach town she's come to love. Her gallery is thriving and she's making friends, but the secret of her past hangs heavy over her head.

And the past just won't let her go. Her ex keeps sending letters that yank her back into the terrible events that ruined the life she'd thought was near perfect. Her daughter has a budding relationship with a boy she knows nothing about. There's so much uncertainty in spite of the good she's found in Sunset Beach.

When her friend's brother asks her out on a date, she just can't find the courage to say yes. He's handsome and confident and most women would be over the moon that he showed interest. Stella isn't ready, especially with the other worries on her mind.

Juggling the past, present, and future is a struggle Stella isn't handling well. Maybe a new start isn't all it's cracked up to be. Can Stella can find the courage to confront her ex and the issues from the past? Will she finally accept that her daughter has a right to grow up? If so, she just might be able to grab the future she deserves.

Charlotte Golding

Grab your copy now to keep reading the Sunrise Beach
series!

**Living for Today on Amazon**

———

# About the Author

Charlotte Golding has always loved women's fiction - she inherited that love from her mother. Actually, her love of reading started at an early age because her mom read to her every day. What an amazing legacy to instill a love of reading in your children.

Charlotte started out writing historical romance and enjoyed it so much. The research was fun, though there was always a rabbit hole to swallow her up. That's one of the truths of a historical writer.

The call of women's fiction wouldn't go away. So here she is, in the world of women's relationships, family drama, and strong female characters. And she loves it!

Charlotte is a southern girl at heart. She left the south at times over the years, but came back as soon as possible to the place she knows she belongs.

www.ingramcontent.com/pod-product-compliance
Lightning Source LLC
Chambersburg PA
CBHW020337160726
47992CB00004B/1875